# The Slightly True Story of Cedar B. Hartley
## (who planned to live an unusual life)

Martine Murray was born in Melbourne and still lives
there. She started writing because she thought it would
be a good idea to learn a practical skill like typing.
Apart from discovering a lot about waitressing, cooking
rice and yoga, she has spent most of her time studying
impractical things (like art, acrobatics and dance). She
doubts she'll study anything else, since she'd like to find
a normal job one day, so she can buy a new car with
air-conditioning. Martine still spends time walking with
dogs, hanging upside down in the park and making
things up. This is her first novel.

The slightly true story of

# Cedar B. Hartley

(who planned to live
an unusual life)

**Martine Murray**

MACMILLAN CHILDREN'S BOOKS

First published 2003 by Macmillan Children's Books

This edition published 2004 by Macmillan Children's Books
a division of Macmillan Publishers Limited
20 New Wharf Road, London N1 9RR
Basingstoke and Oxford
www.panmacmillan.com

Associated companies throughout the world

ISBN 0 330 41543 3

1 3 5 7 9 8 6 4 2

A CIP catalogue record for this book is available from
the British Library.

Typeset by Intype Libra Ltd
Printed and bound in Great Britain by Mackays of Chatham plc, Kent

For my brother Cam,
who is wayward and lovely,
for my friend Nicole, who is amazing,
and for Nige, who taught me
to walk on my hands

## Warning

Cedar B. Hartley would like to advise all readers
against trying out the balance positions in this
book, unless you have someone experienced to help.
Otherwise you may bump your head
or get a very sore bottom.

# Chapter 1

There are only two places to muck around, where I live – in the street or down by Merri Creek. If you had a horse there would be absolutely nowhere to put it because, apart from the footy oval, which is shorn like a carpet, all the ground is taken up by streets with rows of houses on each side. Each house has a garden which it wears like its own particular hairstyle. The Bartons' is very magnificent and correct, with box hedges, a shaved rectangle of lawn and a cement drive-way full of clean cars. Ours is wild, yellowed and weedy, with NO JUNK MAIL written in black texta on the mailbox. Next door, Mrs Trinka's is flouncy, with ornamentals and puffs of blue hydrangea. At the Motts' house there's a slope of grass that you can roll down, but it makes you itchy after a while. There are trees, of course, mainly paperbarks and plane trees, and two hedges, but nowhere to swim – not unless you make friends with Harold Barton who has a swimming pool out the back. But I wouldn't want to do that. Harold has dirty magazines under his bed, and he sneers.

Doesn't matter, there's still a lot you can do in our street. Everything happens after school and before dinner. That's when you go out with your dog or your skateboard or your secret plan. There's a spilling – kids come tumbling out of doors and fences, with blobs of jam on their chins and jumbled-up notions in their minds and a loosed-up flop in their strut. We pile onto the street and shoot out a riot of looks and hunches, we sniff about, hook up our notions, pace our minds up and down the street and wait for something to happen, because something always will. It's like a chemical rule – mix up kids on a long slope of bitumen with bikes and boards and dogs and a lazy lurking need to mess with the lattice of rules that looms over you at school, and before long something happens.

To be honest, Harold Barton wouldn't make friends with me, anyway, because I'm not pretty enough. He only talks to the pretty girls. Sixteen-year-olds with shapes sticking out. Girls like Marnie Aitkin who wears hipsters and says, 'Oh really?' to absolutely anything you might say.

'Hey Marnie, they say tonight the stars will fall out of the sky, and if you stick out your tongue one might land on it, and if you swallow it then you become a star yourself.'

'Oh sure,' she says, 'very funny.' That's the other thing she says. 'Oh sure'.

It doesn't always happen with a bang in our street. Sometimes things sizzle into action. Sometimes you just stumble onto a game, and if a game's got legs you can play it again the next day and the next. Like the game we play in the carpark spaces at the train station; that's a game where still, even now, someone will say, 'Wanna go down the carpark on the bikes?' And we might go.

But in the end it all depends on who's out there and how the mix is made. Since the older ones (like Hoody Mott who can play French horn, and Roland Glumac, and Sarah with the legwarmers) go lurk in bedrooms and do homework, or smoke or talk on the telephone, you hardly see them much, and that leaves Harold Barton to decide who's in and who's not. That's because he has the swimming pool and the biggest house. So he acts like he knows everything, and kids believe him because kids like swimming. What's more, his parents let him do whatever he wants, so you can eat waffles and chocolate at his house, or watch R-rated television, or play Powderfinger as loud as hell on the stereo. The main attraction at Harold's is the back bungalow, because it's a permanent parent-free zone. The Year Twelve girls, like Marnie Aitkin and Aileen Shelby, go there. Barnaby says they play Strip Jack Naked. Barnaby's my older brother. Everyone liked him the most, but now he's gone. He got sent away. That leaves Harold.

Kids all have their own ways of grouping around and ganging-up and jiggling and tweaking and overhauling the ordinary state of things. Sometimes action surges down to the creek or trickles out across Westgarth Street or Hutton Street. Sometimes it scoops you up like an avalanche would if you were standing in the way. Sometimes it leaves behind small puddles, possibilities, promises . . . perhaps a new friend with a good bike.

As for me, I avoid the main swell of street action and drift towards the puddles. A puddle isn't just what's left behind, although sometimes you may feel like it is. A puddle of people is full of rich deposits.

Take my puddle, for example. There are normally three of us in it, though sometimes you could say four or five. First there's me, and I'm exasperating and potentially infamous. My name is Lana Monroe. I have red hair and I'm twelve, almost thirteen, which means I'm not old enough to be invited to play in Harold's bungalow but I'm too old for making water bombs or playing kumquat wars. That's for kids.

My name isn't really Lana Monroe, I just like you to think it might be, since it has a famous kind of ring to it. My real name is Cedar B. Hartley; Cedar because it's a type of tree and my mother was in a deep hippy phase when I was born. Hippies hinge a lot of their strong feelings on trees, and often give their children names like River and Marigold. Harold Barton screws up his nose at my name. 'What kind of a name is that?' he says. Harold suffers from a lack of imagination, says to my mother. She calls me Cedy when she's in a good mood and Cedar when I'm in trouble.

Then there's my friend Caramella Zito who lives directly opposite me. She's almost twelve, but not quite, so that makes me way older than her. There's no lawn in her garden, just beds of beans and tomatoes and fennel, and also geraniums and an olive tree, and a real grape vine around the side. Caramella's parents are very short and they don't speak much English, but they give my mother bunches of grapes and sometimes a persimmon, which is the most spectacular fruit I have ever tried. Caramella is extremely shy, especially when she has pimples and Harold calls her Zito the Zit Face. She's just a little bit chubby and wears a cross on a necklace. Caramella is a brilliant artist, though only I know that. Sometimes she doesn't come outside into the street, so I go to her place.

Then there's Ricci. Ricci is about fifty or sixty, so that makes her by far the oldest. She lives next door to Caramella Zito's and even though she's really Yugoslavian she can speak Italian. So she's chummy with Caramella's parents. Sometimes, though, she swears about them. 'Bloody Italians,' she says. Ricci knows all kinds of things that other people don't know. She can look at a rainbow and tell you what it thinks.

'Ah look,' she says, pointing at the rainbow, 'a good season for berries and wine.'

She lives with a fluffy white dog called Bambi, who's about twice as big as a slipper. In her house there are a lot of flowers and stuffed animals and blown-up blurry photos of her in disco tights when she was young. Her hair is frizzy and blonde and she doesn't like Australia, but she likes having a house. Her husband died a while ago so she has to take Valium, which makes her feel better and then worse again. Sometimes she works at the bakery, but mostly she walks about in the street talking to one person about another person and spreading sunflower seeds or cape gooseberry cuttings. Here's what Ricci looks like:

Ricci

Sometimes in my puddle there's also Hailey and her little brother Jean-Pierre, who mainly hoons around on a bike that's way too big for him. They live on the corner in a house with a tall wood fence which is old with some bits missing, so you can peek through. Their father drives a Silvertop taxi. He's huge and dark and he comes from Syria. Sometimes you can hear strange exultant music coming from their house. Once, I looked through the gap in the fence to see if there were people in turbans playing flutes and bongos, but it was just a ghetto blaster on a card table under a lemon tree, with the whole family, even a few grandmothers (in black head scarves, not turbans), sitting around eating McDonald's. Hailey and Jean-Pierre don't like Harold because he calls them Lebbos.

But just about everyone else in the street seems to want to muck around with Harold. Even Barnaby once did.

# Chapter 2

It was really because of Stinky that everything changed.
What I really mean is everything started.

Stinky is my dog. Once he was mine and Barnaby's, but
now he's just mine. He's only a sweet shaggy old mutt but
I love him like mad. This is what he looks like:

stinky

Barnaby found him down by the creek last year and
brought him home saying, 'Phew, he's sure a stinky old
bastard isn't he?' Mum was frantic, wringing her hands and
sighing because Stinky jumped up on the couch straightaway and left dirty paw prints everywhere. Dirt tends to
make all mothers anxious.

When Stinky lifted his little hairy leg on the clean
washing pile, Mum actually groaned. She looked at Barnaby

and said, 'He's not staying.' But Barnaby talked her into it.
He could do that, because he was the only male in the
house so Mum loved him an awful lot.

My mum works with accident victims and she doesn't
come home till dinner time, so it's usually just me and
Stinky at home together after school. I shovel down a bowl
of Weet-Bix and then we go out, either to the street or
down the creek.

One day I got home from school and Stinky wasn't
there. No one wriggling, stomping, huffing or burning
around to find a sock to put in his mouth, no one acting
like he'd been waiting around all day for me to come home,
no one pleased to see me, no one I was pleased to see. The
house felt thuddingly empty and unnaturally still, like a tree
that isn't moving its leaves in the wind. It was all wrong,
I could tell. I yelled at the sad grey old walls with the
wobbly windows and the Bruegel picture of peasants
working in a yellow field, but nothing happened. I wanted
a warm wriggling and a shouting, like I hear coming from
Caramella Zito's house, and sizzle smells like I smell at
Ricci's house, or even Barnaby hollering out a song
on his guitar.

And then I was sad; not purely sad, more murkily so.
I felt as if there was nothing to count on or touch, nothing
except echoes and shadows and disappearances. Life had
turned to quicksand and the faint yellow light in the kitchen
spread out towards me like the ghostly breath of lives that

had left. Definitely spooky. And all because Stinky wasn't
there. Which goes to show how much difference a little
furry friend can make.

Our kitchen slopes downwards. There are big holes
in the floor where you can see the dirt underneath, and in
the middle of the kitchen there's a wooden table with one
shonky sloping leg that you need to kick every now and
then to make it straight. It's a good kitchen, though, because
the slope makes it like a boat, and there's a chunk of outside
coming in through the window. You can see a canopy of
oak leaves whispering in the blue air while you eat your
Weet-Bix, and you can hear a frenzied chorus of myna birds
and parrots, arguing over the acorns. The kitchen joins
another small room where there's a fat old couch and a
tellie. To get this room warm you have to light the oven in
the kitchen and leave the door open, but since there was no
one to feel snug or lazy or buzzy with, I couldn't even be
bothered lighting the oven. I slumped down on the couch
and tugged out handfuls of the muddy grape-coloured
stuffing which bulged out of the holes, and thought about
how Barnaby had gone, and Granma, and how I didn't have
a dad and how my mum wasn't home, and how even Stinky
had run away. Boy I hate it when people leave. Maybe I'll
leave too, I thought. Get on a train and go interstate. Just
to be the one who went. I didn't, though, because strange
murders are committed in Adelaide, and Sydney is for people
who tan easily and every other state is too far away and too

hot. I went and asked Ricci if she'd seen Stinky. Ricci knows everything that's going on.

'No, I not see Stinky,' she squawked, because Ricci always squawks. 'You try the creek?'

'Nope, not yet.'

She slapped my shoulder and said, 'You go look. I go ask the boys.'

The boys are two greyish men who live together in the neatest whitest house in the street. They have opium poppies and iceberg roses in their front garden and a white path leading to their door.

'Go, don't worry,' said Ricci, giving me a shove. She always gives orders and shoves. She doesn't mean it badly, though. It's just that she doesn't bother with suggestions and reasons because it's too much trouble to find all those words that reasons need. Ricci is very economical. She grows all her own vegetables, and makes soup out of weeds and turkey necks. Sometimes she comes over to my house with turkey soup, and sighs and puts her hands on her hips.

'Where your mother?' she says. 'Cedar, here I wash these dishes and you dry.'

And once she starts cleaning you can't stop her. She even scrubs out the cupboards and wipes the stove. It drives me mad, but afterwards I feel relieved because the house can seem snarly when it's grubby. Then it gets this sweet pure look, like a home on tellie, when the stove is clean.

*    *    *

I went down to the creek and I yelled out 'Stinky' all the
way. I saw Marnie Aitkin and Aileen Shelby, because they
always go about in a pair.

'What are you yelling that out for, Cedar? Did you do
a fart?' said Aileen, who always has a smart-ass thing to say.
Marnie giggled into her well manicured hand. Aileen's eyes,
I noticed, were close together – they had the look of a
snake.

'I lost my dog Stinky. Have you seen him?'

Aileen shook her head.

'Oh really?' said Marnie. 'We're going to Harold's house.'

'Well have fun,' I said, but I don't think I meant it. Those
girls made me feel not quite right.

☆   ☆   ☆

I didn't find Stinky that afternoon, and he didn't come home
the next day. Caramella came over to show me the bandage
round her ankle. She sprained it trampolining, because she's a
bit of a hefalump when it comes to sporty things. I tried to
be sympathetic about the sprain but I was feeling more sorry
for myself. And Caramella was happy about having an injury,
anyway, especially because her dad had to drive her to
school.

I decided to make a lost dog notice. I got Caramella to
draw a picture of Stinky because she's much better at
drawing than I am. This is what it looked like:

### Lost dog.
He is small and shaggy and looks a bit like this

answers to name Stinky,
likes bones and chasing rabbits and when
he goes in the creek he smells a bit,
but is very friendly and well loved and missed.
Unique Reward offered.
Please call 9380 0195.

I wasn't sure what the unique reward would be, but I thought I could get some of Ricci's Russian sunflowers because they're enormous and make you think prehistoric fairytale thoughts. Ricci asked one of the boys to photocopy the notice for me at work. The boys love Ricci. She looks after their garden for them when they go to Thailand for holidays, and they gave her a microwave oven for Christmas but she won't use it because she says it kills the life force.

I stuck the notice up on telephone poles all around the block and down by the oval. Then I started up again with my moping, and Caramella limped and Ricci squawked, 'Don't worry darling, Stinky come back. He's smart dog.'

# Chapter 3

Actually, even I ran away once. It was on my twelfth birthday. I ran away because everyone forgot it was my birthday. I was alternately slouching and hopping on one leg, waiting for someone to notice, but they were all busy making plans and talking on the phone. See, I was born on a special day, the last day of the year: 31 December, 1988, to be precise. Problem is, it's a special day that belongs to everyone, not just me. New Year's Eve it's called. Imagine if you had to share your birthday with the whole world. It's a bummer, 'cause on your birthday you want to feel special. You want to own the day.

Now, I'm generally not a selfish person, but you can't help feeling a bit blue when everyone is so busy celebrating your birthday that they actually forget about you. Me, Cedar B. Hartley. Born on the last day of the year. Bee- and bird-lover. Bound to be infamous. Bad at maths but good at other things, like jumping and making up games. Me. How could they have forgotten? That's what was mooning around in my mind. Even Barnaby had forgotten. All excited about a dumb party he was going to at Harold Barton's, of course.

I kicked at the ground and practised head stands to draw some attention to myself. When that didn't work, I faked a thought: *Well, who needs them anyway?* I said to myself. *Me and Stinky, we'll go have our own celebration.*

So I went down the milkbar and bought a box of Orange Thins, the ones Mum has for after dinner parties. Polite people only take one. Since Mum is training me to be polite, I'm only allowed one. Each chocolate comes in its own little chocolate-coloured envelope, just so as you know they're special. Sophisticated chocolates, that's what I wanted for my twelfth birthday. Well, not really. I'd actually been dropping hints about a horse. Hints like: *I know where there might be a paddock* (which is a big lie). *Oh I wish I had a horse, I'd be a better child if I only had a horse* (with big sigh accompanying).

I don't think Mum got the hint. I guess I knew it was a lot to hope for. Anyway Orange Thins are easier to take with you when you run away, and I had a whole box just for me and Stinky. It was, after all, my first day of being a twelve-year-old, which is as close as you can get to almost being a teenager, and I wanted to do something that proved just how grown-up I was.

To tell you the truth, I didn't feel any different. I don't think you ever do. I think one day you just become sixty or seventy, and it must be a shock to be so old because it's still

the same you on the inside; it's just that all the outside of
you has got wrinkled from the weather. When I'm that old
I'll still sneak an Orange Thin, I know it. Actually, that's got
to be the best thing about being old; you don't have to
worry about getting holes in your teeth any more 'cause
your teeth are already rotten or gone or replaced. And you
don't have to wait for someone to let you eat a chocolate,
you can just go right ahead and eat five and a half if you
want. Sophisticated ones, too, not cobbers or rollos or
freckles. Orange Thins. They sound kind of restrained and
elegant, like an Oriental lady in a silk dress.

So I went to the bridge and stuffed my face and gave half
to Stinky, because it's no fun if you can't gloat with someone
else. We sat under the bridge, and then we tried to stay out
for as long as possible to make sure Mum and Barnaby
noticed that we had run away. I pictured them sitting at the
kitchen table feeling terribly bad about forgetting my
birthday; Mum sobbing into her coffee, and Barnaby
slumped in a state of deep regret, and besieged by thoughts
of what a dear, sweet, deserving sister I was, feeling
compelled to discuss, at great length, ways he and Mum
could possibly make it up to me by pitching in for an extra
good present (large fast white horse). That's what I imagined.

When Stinky and I finally went home again, Mum
rushed up to me and was all sorry about forgetting my
birthday. She hadn't been sobbing, though, and she just gave
me a toilet bag with Oil of Ulan in it. Oil of Ulan is pink

moisturiser, for rubbing on your skin so you don't get
wrinkles. Mum said that since I was almost a teenager I had
to start looking after my skin. Barnaby had already gone to
the party (which turned out to be a dud rage anyway). He
left a note and a book on my bed. The book was called *D is
for Dog*. The note said:

> Happy Birthday Cedy Blue. I have a thought
> for you. Life is a hungry ocean. Leave nothing
> untouched. Love Barnaby.

There was a drawing of the ocean with it. Barnaby always
does drawings with his cards. He secretly likes to think of
himself as a bit of a poet, but I think he was in a rush when
he wrote that. He calls me Cedy Blue because there's a tree
in the Botanic Gardens called an Atlas Blue Cedar, and
Barnaby says that must be the tree I was named after and
that's where our mum and dad did it, right there under the
blue tree. But I think he's making it up because it isn't a
very intimate tree. It looks like it should be on a mountain
where there are mooses. When I asked Mum, she said it was
a load of nonsense, and that Barnaby has an overactive
imagination.

atlas blue cedar with a moose

I tried to be pleased about the moisturiser, but I could tell that Mum had just gone and bought it at the chemist, because it wasn't wrapped up. The best part of a present is the moment when you begin to unwrap it, when you don't quite know and you are full of hope and anticipation.

Well, Oil of Ulan wouldn't have even slightly resembled a horse even if it was wrapped up. *It's the thought that counts*, I kept saying to myself. But I wasn't that excited about having to look after my skin. So far, it had looked after itself just fine.

a horse wrapped up.

Come to think of it, I don't really believe that stuff about it being the thought that counts. It's only half true, because what if the thought isn't a very thoughtful thought, like how my mum always gives Ricci a box of Quality Street chocolates? Now, if she was being really thoughtful she might have noticed that Ricci is nearly always on a diet. She might have given her a book about tofu instead, or new shoes, because Ricci loves shoes, especially if they're silver or gold.

And there are certainly more positive things than skin problems to think about when you become a teenager. Like what about freedom? What about being allowed to do things on your own? What about getting smarter? By the time I'm as old as Mum, I'm going to be damn smart. She has to do a lot of thinking for accident victims, because they have acquired brain injuries (which is the right way to say that their brains got messed up by some kind of accident involving a big bang on the head). So her thinking quota is just about used up by the time she gets home and she can't be thinking thoughtful thoughts about me and Ricci, and Caramella with a sprained ankle.

One time, I asked Mum if she thought I would be famous.

'Cedar my love, you'll be infamous.'

'What's that?'

'Infamous is more famous than famous,' she said with a sigh, because I exasperate her with questions when she's tired.

I don't know what I'll be infamous for; certainly not for geometry or invention of inventions, because I'm not good at straight lines or electricity.

# Chapter 4

Anyway, it didn't feel right walking down the creek or mucking around in the street without Stinky. I stayed inside and read *D is for Dog*. It tells you everything you might need to know in alphabetical order: false teeth, field spaniels, fits, flatulence, fleas, foreign bodies . . . I'd never even thought about false teeth for dogs. You'd think a book like that, with dental advice and stuff, would also have a part about lost dogs. I figure there are a lot more homeless dogs than there are dogs wanting some new teeth. My grandmother has false teeth. I found them once in a glass of water. She used to live with us, but then she died of old age. Actually this was Granma's house, and we came to live with her because before that we were living in a small place. It was better when she was here, because she and I used to eat boysenberry ripple ice-cream together. Also, she never got cross. She just wanted to brush my hair.

teeth inside water

Lucky I was lurking around inside thinking about Granma's false teeth, because that was when the phone call came.

'Hello, it's Cedar speaking.'

'Hi, I'm ringing 'bout the dog.' It was a boy's voice, not a roaring or sneering kind of a boy's voice, more like the voice of a river running steadily by.

'Stinky? Did you find him?'

'I think so.'

'Is he okay? Does he have a red collar?'

'Yep.' There was a pause. I could hear him breathe in and out again.

'Where did you find him?'

'Down by the Merri Creek.'

'Do you think I could come and see?' I asked. There was another pause.

'I can meet you on the oval near where you put the lost dog sign,' he said.

'Okay. Soon?'

'Fifteen minutes?' said the river voice.

'Okay, see ya then,' I said, and hung up. Oops, forgot to

ask his name. I checked in the mirror to see how I looked. Cedar B. Hartley's face looked back at me. Not quite Lana Monroe, not quite famous or completely knowledgeable, just a hopeful grin and a halo of red curly hair. I tried out an intelligent expression, but it didn't work. I flared my nostrils to give more shape to the nose and then I stuck my pinkies in and growled. My mood had suddenly gone from moochy to loony. The house was full of light and I didn't care that there were big holes in the lino. I grabbed a banana and set out to bring Stinky home.

## Chapter 5

The sky had a serious grey look. There wasn't anyone down by the creek except the rabbit man. I call him the rabbit man, but he doesn't look or act like a rabbit. Doesn't have long ears or a lot of children. Actually, I can't remember why I call him that. I just do. Sometimes in your mind you call someone something just because it tickles you softly to call them that.

the rabbit man

The rabbit man is old and Italian. He has a walking stick, and he wears a blue shirt done up at the collar, and braces with corduroys, and sneakers. Corduroy on an old person is always a good sign of sturdiness. Besides, he loves dogs. His dog is an old hobbling black-and-tan dog called Diva. They go together very well.

'But where your dog?' he said, waving his walking stick in the air with some enthusiasm. The rabbit man speaks very loudly and clearly. He says each word with much deliberation, as if he was planting it inside you. When he says 'Diva' he squeezes out the Di and hammers open the va, like Deeee va. I usually love to listen to him plant words, but this time I was in a hurry to get to the oval and hang over the pole.

'He's at the oval. Gotta go get him.'

'He your best friend. Your dog your best friend,' called out the rabbit man. He says that every time you see him. He likes to bend down and hold out his hand to every dog that passes by. He showed me that. Always let a dog come to you, that way you won't scare him, he says.

Some people are scared of dogs. I like to ride my bike up Sydney Road and watch all the Arabian ladies shrink inside their head-wraps as Stinky runs past them. I know I shouldn't, but I figure it's good practice for those scared ladies to see how a dog won't bite your knee or curse you. Dogs are even nicer than some people. Like me. After all, I'm the one who's amusing myself at the scared ladies' expense. Not Stinky. He doesn't even notice them. Not unless they've got a sausage.

sausage and sausage dog

It started to rain. I don't have anything against rain – it's good for the farmers and all – but I just didn't fancy getting wet. Sometimes I can get over it. I can just turn my face up to the sky and say, 'Come on then, go ahead, wet me.' Then I can enjoy the wet feeling. I even want to see just how completely soaked I can get. I want to be more wet by the rain than anyone has ever been before. But I didn't feel like it that day, not at all. Getting sopping wet is only fun when you know you can run home and peel off your clothes and slither into a hot bath. But when you're on your way to meet a river-voiced boy who found your dog, you don't want to drip all over his shoes.

So, I headed for the cooing bridge. Stinky looked pretty funny when he got wet. His hair stuck up everywhere. This is what he looked like:

stinky when wet

The cooing bridge is quite ugly on top because cars run over it, and quite ugly underneath because there's graffiti and pigeon shit everywhere and a dirty grey hollowed-out feeling. If I was doing graffiti, at least I would want to write a magnificent thought or draw a picture of a bird going fishing, but all you see under the bridge is words like AKS.

Who knows what that means? Painted in red on the pillars holding the bridge up it says PAT on one and CARY on the other. (Not a great point of departure except that it makes me imagine two blokes who used to play footy together and now they're going bald and making salami which they sell to delicatessens in Brunswick.) Barnaby says graffiti is about 'tags'(kind of personal logos), but I think it's just like how dogs like to wee on walls. Boy dogs and boy kids like to leave a mark.

So, the only way to make the bridge beautiful is to close your eyes and listen to it coo. It's the pigeons who are cooing, of course, not the bridge, though if you didn't see the pigeons hidden up underneath it, you could think it was the bridge. I try to work out what they might be saying. So far, I know this much – it's a tender and mushy sentiment like, *Oh my darling, let me make your nest more comfortable. There, shall I give your little bird claws a rub? What a good bridge we live in. Would you like an Orange Thin?*

Cooing translation is not as stupid as you might think, because I once heard of a monk called Francis in Italy who could talk to animals and birds. I can almost speak dog and I'm not even a monk. But I know what Stinky is saying. I understand tail language. Round and round tail movement, for example, is very pleased, whereas upwards pointing is a question, like *Who's there? Are you a rabbit? Can I come?* There is also a language in his eyes. Tail language and eye language go together.

*a dog speaking dog*

Stinky can almost speak human, too. At home we can't say the word 'walk', because it makes Stinky go crazy. He starts barking and jumping with excitement, and that hurts my mum's head. So instead we say, 'I'm going for a "w".' I don't know why, but he hasn't worked that one out yet. Talking is one thing, but spelling is another.

*bird tenderness*

There I was, thinking about nice things like bird tenderness and dog spelling when who should intrude on my nicely cooed-out mind but Harold Barton.

'Well look who's here,' said the sneery voice of Harold Barton. He was standing there, panting like a dog. Next to him were Patrick Murphy and Frank Somebody. They were all wet. Rain dripped off Harold's back-to-front-cap and trickled down his neck.

'Heard from your brother?' he said.

'Nope,' I said, looking at Patrick Murphy and wondering if it was him who wrote PAT.

'Barnaby's a weirdo,' said Harold, putting his lips in an ugly shape. 'Anyway, whatcha doing here sittin' under a bridge on your own, Cedar? I don't get you Hartleys.'

Harold thought anyone who didn't flock around him was weird, especially if they liked their own company. I considered telling him that I was translating bird, but I thought better of it and ignored the question completely. Best not to give him too much to go on. I knew Harold had secretly admired Barnaby quite a lot, which is not surprising since Barnaby is charming and girls go crazy for him. It was a lie that we hadn't heard from him, because he sends postcards. Usually they're just a bit of cardboard cut out of a box, with a texta drawing on the front and two sentences on the back. Like this:

> dear Mum and Cedy, day after day, up here beating my wings and staggering, imagine the sky and how it wonders.

But I wasn't going to tell Harold about that, firstly because he suffers from a lack of imagination and so he wouldn't appreciate it, but also because I have a feeling that something funny went down. Barnaby wouldn't tell me what, but I know it had something to do with Barnaby being sent away.

'Harold, I know you got Barnaby into trouble, I just know,' I said.

'Did not. Anyway, Barnaby deserved it.'

'Deserved what?' I narrowed my eyes suspiciously and Harold narrowed his eyes back, and then he went all American-movie, putting his hand to his heart and looking about at his buddies with a well practised poor-me look in his eye. Harold Barton is the most expert worm I ever met. He made out it was him that was getting the bum steer, just so he wouldn't have to answer my leading question.

'Hey dudes, Cedar's coming on all raw prawn at me. Just because her brother's a weirdo. Hey, Der-brain, face the facts. You and your brother are weirdos. And you got no dad.'

I didn't think this really deserved a response from me, especially since Frank Somebody was already responding with a lot of embarrassed grunting and shuffling. (I can't think of Frank's surname because Frank isn't the kind of person you think about much.) Patrick Murphy changed the topic.

'C'mon, let's get to the footy,' he said, jerking his head in the direction of the oval. Patrick was dead keen on football. He was what I call a meaty bloke. He crossed his chunky arms over his chest. 'Reckon we should make a run for it.'

'Yeah, okay, let's go.' Harold pulled out a pair of dark sunglasses and wiped off the rain with his T-shirt. 'See ya, weirdo,' he said, without even looking at me, and then all three of them jogged off.

I had to go as well, but I lagged behind them, feeling a bit droopy and doomed because there would be a crowd

of people on the oval for the footy match, and because
Harold had called me Der-brain, which really gets on my
high-and-mighty nerves since I quite value my brain, thank
you very much, and I know my brain would never stoop so
low as to tease people for not having fathers or mothers or
swimming pools, either. I should have said something.
Something like what Uncle John might have said; *Harold
Barton, you don't know nothing, you wouldn't even know if the
Salvation Army was up your bum playing the Dead March*. But I
never remember things like that. I never even remember
good jokes. Except the one about the trembling wreck, or
the dog – which reminded me, I was about to find Stinky,
the hairy chap, my favourite beast. Only now that all those
people would be on the oval, how was I going to find the
river-voiced boy?

   Trudge trudge I went, muttering and splattering in my
mind. But the rain started to slow down and slivers of sun
glittered on the wet leaves, and I must have trudged that
grumpy feeling right out of me and right into the mud
because I could feel something else rising up, all fluttery like
a big gulp of lemonade. It made me skip, but only for a little
bit, because I wouldn't want anyone to see me skip. Only
little kids skip.

## Chapter 6

The footy was in full swing. I swept my eyes around the edge
of the oval, following the rail. Groups of spectators huddled
under the trail of willow trees that stood by the creek. People
held newspapers over their heads and yelled and pummelled
the air with fists. A crowd by the clubhouse stood in clumps
under the tin roof; some of them were wearing team stripes. I
couldn't see Stinky anywhere, or Harold and the gang (thankfully), so I decided to practise my pole positions, because
otherwise I might just have stood there imagining ways of
luring one hundred rats into Harold Barton's bedroom.

Firstly I got into bird position, like this:

This obviously requires great strength
and balance. You need to become bird-like.
You stretch your toes away from the tip of
your head and then arch upwards and press
your heart forwards. If you try it out,
make sure you hang on until you find your balance.
Barnaby can't do this. He hates it that I can. Barnaby thinks

bird position

he should be always better than me because he's older and
bigger. He pretends he isn't interested in the pole positions,
but I know he's just jealous 'cause he can't do them. The
second position is bat position:

You just let your head dip
down and your legs fly up. I cross
my legs over and let my head dangle.

bat position

It's especially good for getting a different slant on life. People
walking look much better when you are upside-down. They
go loopy and bouncy, like astronauts on another planet.

Then there's the bridge. It looks like this:

Try cooing in this position and maybe
a pigeon will nest under your arm.

I was hanging in the bat position,
vaguely watching the footy match

bridge position

upside-down. It looked much better. There was a dad
standing nearby who kept screaming, 'Come on Zebras!
Get on the ball!'

When the other team got a goal, all the Zebras hung
their heads. One guy punched the goal post with his fist.
I felt sorry for them. I'm glad I don't have to play footy.
Sometimes Barnaby tried to get me to have a kick with
him, but I don't get it. I don't get how you can know which
direction that egg-shaped ball is going to bounce. It's
capricious. And I can't kick it right. Barnaby says it's because
I'm a girl. If being a boy means you have to play footy, then
I'm glad I'm a girl. Barnaby was the best footy player out of

everyone. Even Harold Barton's dad said so when he was watching a game of kick-to-kick in the street. That made Harold sulk. I saw him. He went red and his mouth puffed up like a goldfish. And I gloated quietly, from my tree. Sometimes I'm a secret meanie.

football bouncing capriciously

That dad was getting all worked up and pinkish in the face. He said, 'Geez! They're playing like a bunch of women.' I shot him a glare (since I'm a stark raving feminist) but because I was upside-down I don't think it got to him. An upside-down glare can't hit the spot with directness, especially when the man is fat which makes things bounce off instead of slicing in. When Harold Barton gives me a dirty look it glides right in because I'm skinny.

'Why you hanging upside-down?' It was the river voice asking me. I saw brown hair. A boy. I could almost see up his nose.

'I'm training,' I said, looking through his legs for some sign of Stinky.

'What for?' He was wearing a T-shirt with some writing on it. I couldn't read it upside-down, so I flipped back up the right way.

'The Bat Pole Championship.' His T-shirt said Wangaratta Jazz Festival 1993. Not a bad thing to have on your T-shirt, not like Harold's which always have fashion logos on them.

The boy scrunched up his nose. I could tell he was dubious.

'What's a Bat Pole Championship?'

Fair question, I thought, and for a moment I didn't know how to reply since I'd only just made it up right then.

'What's the Wangaratta Jazz Festival?' I said. It's a trick I've worked out. When you can't think of an answer, stall for time – ask another question.

'It's a jazz festival at Wangaratta. My dad got the T-shirt, not me.'

'Is your dad a musician?'

'Nope, not really.' I hadn't decided if I was dying to know about other people's fathers, or if I was dying not to know. Before I could stop it, there were images filling my mind – a dad with a T-shirt on, casually humming and saying, 'Wanna go for a drive?' I frowned those dad images away.

'Well, did you bring Stinky?' I said.

His eyebrows went up and his eyes smiled. 'Are you Cedar?'

'Yeah, I'm Cedar. I'm wet, I know. Don't worry, I'm better when I'm dry.' I swiftly ran my hand through my hair to check if it had become a post-rain frizz ball.

'You were supposed to be by the pole.' His hair was short and plain and not fussed-over at all.

'Oops, I forgot about that.'

'Well, Stinky's tied up over there.' He pointed back behind the clubhouse and there, curled up under a Melaleuca tree, was Stinky. Lying quite contentedly, it seemed; not a sign of any sense of loss or yearning for me.

'Stinky boy!' I yelled. And up he stood, wagging his stumpy little tail and doing such an excited continuous stomp that I was thankfully relieved of the need to prove that he was in fact my lost dog.

'He looks happy to see you.'

Stinky, once set free, raced between us, yelping in confused excitement. The boy was a dog person, obviously.

The way I figure it, the world is made of two types of people – dog people and cat people. If you drew a line down the middle and said all dog people on one side and cat people on the other, then the dog side of the world would be chaotic and muddy, an exuberant unparticular big kind of a place with many trees. The cat side would be clean and deliberate and full of sunny patches and silk couches. I belong to the dog side, so does my mum, and even Barnaby. But Marnie Aitkin, she definitely belongs to the cat side. It's the coral coloured fingernails. So does Laura Pinkstone. That's why I knew that Barnaby had gone stupid asking her out, because it wouldn't ever have worked out. Even if Barnaby hadn't been sent away, he and Laura Pinkstone just belong on different sides. Do you think a dog could marry a cat?

world divided in half

I looked carefully at the boy with the river voice. A long neck. Brown skinny arms. Face that looked away.

'Do you play footy?' I said, because I felt I should say something.

'Nup.' He just shrugged.

'Why not?'

'Don't like it much.'

'No, I don't either. It's capricious,' I said, thinking he might be impressed with that word capricious. But he didn't seem to notice. He was still patting Stinky. I could tell by the way he patted that he definitely had the ways of a dog person. Cat people pat from above with little puffy, pattery pats, and they pull their face away so as not to smell dog smell. When I pat Stinky I like to get really close. I like to put my face in his ears and smell him.

'You're a dog person, aren't you?' I said.

'No, I'm a bird person.' He said it without even thinking, as if I'd asked him a normal question. Well, I have to admit, that threw me for a moment. I thought there were only two sides to the world. But I was wrong. There's also the sky. That's the mystery that surrounds it all.

'Yeah? What makes you a bird person?'

He looked at me, as if he was figuring whether I was worth telling or not. His gaze dug into me, all serious and intent, the look in his eyes wide and wild and almost knowing. But what could he know? The eyes were on me as if he was examining me for a defect. It made me fidget. He turned away, jerked his head and laughed. Then he jumped up and grabbed a branch, swung himself up and landed on top of the branch. I have to say it – I was impressed.

And then he did more things, the kind of things I do on the pole, only better. He could swing in and out of all sorts of crazy positions in the tree. He jumped between the branches and got a momentum going so his body could swing up and hook in. I was mad, mad, mad. Mad with wanting to be able to do that too. Mad that he could do that and I couldn't. It seemed almost impossible for someone to move like that, like an animal, as if he knew for sure that he wouldn't fall.

'How did you learn to do that?' I said. There I was, thinking I'd impressed him with my dumb old bat position, when all the time he was much, much better than me. He was still hooked-up in the branches, but he swung down in such a way, like a prince might jump off a horse after winning an important battle. I pretended I didn't notice.

'My dad showed me. When I was a kid.' He poked at the dirt with a stick.

'Lucky you.' I always used to ask my mum to take me to gymnastics classes (especially after I saw the Olympics on tellie), but she said she couldn't take time off work and also we didn't have the money. Once she took me to a jazz ballet class on Saturday in a community hall, but all the other girls were wearing leotards and I felt silly in my trackie dacks.

I thanked him for finding Stinky, and I told him I owed him a reward.

'Nuh, don't worry about it,' he said waving his hand. 'See ya 'round.' Then he walked away. I watched him go for a bit, just to see if he walked like an animal. I liked the way his arms swung. Stinky and I walked home and I let my arms swing up and down, just as if I was about to take off. It was brilliant.

# Chapter 7

When I got home, Mum's hands went straight to her hips
and her lips hit a straight line. The you're-in-trouble
position. It used to make Barnaby cringe and go all quiet.

'Well, where have you been, Cedar?' she said.

'I found Stinky. Look.'

She wasn't happy.

'Did you get wet? You'll catch your death of cold. Go
and take off your clothes.'

She said·it as if she was just stamping a letter, precisely,
with a tight-lipped, end-of-conversation face. I didn't even
get a chance to tell her about the boy who could swing
through trees. So I huffed off upstairs and flopped onto
Barnaby's bed. Just like Barnaby used to do. I put on my
very necessary Stevie Wonder CD and ran a bath. I poured
in the Radox and lay down low with my hair, underneath
the water, floating like weeds. I like to feel mermaidish in
the bath and make things up. *Blame it on the sun, the sun that
doesn't shine, blame it on the wind* . . . sang Stevie, and I

imagined my father, and what he would have showed me if
he hadn't died. I pictured him lifting me up on his shoulders
and sitting me in a tree . . . *but my heart blames it on me . . .*

There's a photo of my dad and me. He's wearing a hat, a
terry towelling fishing hat, and a denim shirt with press studs
that's half open so you can see his chest. He wasn't a fisherman, though. He was a musician. In the photo, I'm just a
one-year-old baby, and I look as unremarkable as just about
any ginger-headed baby you see. He's looking into the camera
and holding me on his shoulders. He's half-laughing and half-
smiling. You can't tell which. But his eyebrows are raised, as
if he is asking someone, 'Is this right, is this what you want?'

*       *       *

Now there's a new puddle, I thought – the bird boy by the
creek. I was hoping I might bump into him again, mainly
because I wanted to learn how to play in trees the way he
could.

I told Caramella about the bird boy, and we practised
hanging upside-down or worming out along branches on
the plane tree in the street. Actually, Caramella just coached
from the ground because her ankle was still sore, and besides
she's too soft and artistic for tree-climbing, but she did make
a top-notch coach. Sometimes I thought I might just stay up
the tree, because I planned to live an unusual life, but it got
too uncomfortable and no one like the bird boy was
noticing anyway. Harold Barton came along with a gang of

his drongo mates, who only want to look up girls' dresses, so I spat on them. Mum grounded me for two days. Ricci brought me over some boiled chicory with egg and said, 'Bloody boys anyway!'

When I was allowed out again, I hung around the oval after school, thinking I might just bump into the boy, because I did owe him a reward, after all. I practised handstands and hung upside-down on the pole counting out cats and dogs and thinking that he might just show up. But he didn't, and after a while I began to think despondent thoughts, like how my nose wasn't refined or how our house was sinking at the foundations. (You can tell because none of the doors close unless you wedge the Iris Murdoch paperback underneath to jam them shut.)

Little Jean-Pierre whizzed past on his bike.

'Hey Cedar, you know what?'

'What?'

'Harold Barton says you've gone batty like your brother, 'cause you hang upside-down. Look what I can do.'

He took his hands off the handles, folded them behind his head and tore off down the track.

Maybe I was turning the world up the other way a bit too much. I went home. There was a card from Barnaby:

Cedy Blue, I saw our dad in a dream. He said, 'Welcome home. Where are your shoes?'
At about 7 o'clock I went for a swim and the sea was black. Imagine the effort the stars made to appear over it.

I got out Mum's Silver Convention record and sang along to *Fly Robin Fly* very loudly in the bathroom – because it sounds better in there. I know another thing I won't be infamous for – singing.

There are two main differences between me and Barnaby. The first is that he's a good singer and I'm a bad singer. The second is that he conceals things and I reveal them. He says I blab. I think he is uncommunicative. He says I'm nosy. I think he suffers from a lack of healthy curiosity. After all, if you don't ask the world questions, then you won't ever work out where the rainbow begins.

Barnaby was five years old when our dad died, so he knew him more than I did and that's why Barnaby can sing. Our dad used to sing songs with him. I always ask Barnaby to tell me stuff about our dad. He says he can't remember, only that Mum had fights with him because he smoked cigarettes, and once he took Barnaby to the beach – just him and Barnaby, and they were there when it was night.

Barnaby has a guitar which he took with him when he went. He used to walk around the house, with it strapped around his shoulder, singing the Memphis blues. He made up words, like:

Oh Cedar can this really be the end?
To be stuck inside a weatherboard with the Brunswick (that's our suburb) blues again.

Mum laughed. And I laughed. And there was a light

feeling in the old house. Then Barnaby got distracted by more serious things, like Nirvana (the band, not the possibility), and girls. And I mean older girls, like Marnie Aitkin, not little sisters like me. Also sometimes he smoked, which I'm not supposed to know about, but I think that made him lazy. He was growing plants on the roof. Secret plants that Mum didn't know about. At least not until that man who cleaned the drainpipes told her. I heard him. He came downstairs in his blue overalls, smelling of sweat and cars and old cigarettes, and he said, 'Ahh, Mrs Hartley, did you know there's marijuana plants growing out on yer roof there?'

Mum brushed her hands downwards on her skirt and she looked funny, as if someone had just asked her to spell a hard word. She sighed and said, 'Thank you, no, I didn't know.'

Our mum is always polite with doctors and workmen and people in the shops.

Boy, Barnaby was in a lot of trouble then! Mum was so angry she could hardly even speak. She just went up, climbed out the window and yanked those plants out herself. Then she stuffed them in the bin. There was dirt trailing from the roof, all the way down the stairs. Normally Mum wouldn't let dirt fall off everywhere like that. Afterwards she vacuumed it up. I could tell she was mad – she was vacuuming like a woman with a bee up her nose. I don't know what she said to him when he got home. The door was closed. But it wasn't long after that when Barnaby went away.

# Chapter 8

For a while I went about trying to concentrate on singing, instead of being upside-down and hoping to meet the bird boy. I wasn't doing that well. I decided it must be because I didn't have a guitar. Stinky and I went hunting around Smith Street looking in the second-hand shops. There weren't any guitars that cost twenty-three dollars, which was all I had, so I gave up and went into Safeway to eat some grapes. Mum doesn't like to shop at Safeway. She says it supports corporate greed and globalisation, so mainly we do our shopping at Friends of the Earth. It's much better, because they have hand-made lavender soap and they're not greedy. What I like about Friends of the Earth is that you fill up your own bags with things, so if you only want a tiny bit of agar agar for making jelly, then you only take a tiny bit, but if you eat loads of muesli and roasted almonds, then you fill a whole big bag up. There are only two reasons to go to Safeway: for garbage bags, and to escape the weather.

Stinky waits outside Safeway while I go in. Usually when I come out again he acts like he hasn't seen me for ages. He wags his whole body. But when I came out this time, there was no little body wagging at me. Stinky was being patted and all I could see was a little furry stomping bum. And who should be doing the patting? Amazing, I thought shaking my red curly head. Life is like that. You try and try and try for something and then, the moment you give up, there it is. The bird boy.

'Hi,' he said, and my face went red.

'Hi,' I said back, wishing I wasn't red. Then we both quickly turned our faces towards Stinky, who is always a great distraction and enjoys the attention. The bird boy was down on one knee.

'Did Stinky recognise you?' I asked.

He stood up and nodded. He was wearing the same T-shirt with some loose-fitting old camel corduroys. He was skinny and rough-looking. I liked the way he looked, like a leaf that had just been tossed by the wind and didn't care.

'I don't know your name.'

'Kite.'

'Kite! That's as strange as Cedar. Were your parents hippies, too?'

'Not really. It's my dad, he's just original. My folks aren't together any more.'

'Mine aren't either.' It felt all right to say that, like he and I had all along been accidentally humming the same song

and we just hit the chorus together. It made me feel
suddenly bold, just because of our mutual parental lack. I
asked him if he wanted to go for a smoothie, since I owed
him anyway.

'Sure. The unique reward, huh?' he said, and laughed, and
his eyes went soft.

☆     ☆     ☆

We went to Soul Food, where they do banana smoothies
with soymilk and the tables are wooden and the waitresses
have nose-rings. When I'm old enough, I might get a nose-
ring. Barnaby has a tattoo of a ladybug on his hip, but Mum
doesn't know about it because she'd be mad. She'd think it
wasn't nice. Barnaby says it's for luck. I said, 'You can't tattoo
luck on your hip,' and he said, 'We'll see.'

Kite and I sat on the high stools at the window table and
watched the people walking up and down Smith Street.
Mum doesn't like me hanging around on Smith Street,
which is exactly what makes me want to hang around there.
I think what she doesn't like is the drug dealers, but they're
just looking for a bloke called Chasen. What I like is
Melissa's, because it's Greek and they do great spinach
triangles for two bucks. And I like the Awareness bookshop,
because the books in it are for telling your fortune. And I
like the Asian shops because they smell funny and the vegetables have warts. There's also a shop called Punctured, where
you can get pierced. And there is also Friends of the Earth.

Blue Lips was pacing up and down the street. Blue Lips never stops. He always looks like he's off to murder someone, or at least give them a good serve, kick in their Hyundai, or stamp on their new shoes. That day he must have been in a good mood, because he wasn't swearing. I don't know why, but Blue Lips always reminds me of Jesus. I think it might be his bare feet and long hair, which is quite beautiful (a bit like Marnie Aitkin's) – golden and wavy and shiny clean. Not what you expect from a crazy guy who never wears a shirt, just leather pants and blue lipstick. He probably gets that lipstick at the Punctured shop.

'Look, Blue Lips has gone in to see Marge,' I said, as Blue Lips turned into the Op Shop.

'Who's Marge?'

'Actually, Marge is a very important person,' I said, accidentally slipping into the philosophical part of my brain. Then I accidentally went and launched into a Life-according-to-Cedar-B.-Hartley theory. Sometimes I can't help myself. I'm accident-prone.

The way I see it, Marge really is important. Not in my fake know-all way, but in an especially true way. Quietly, the no-trumpet-to-blow way. I doubt anyone else in the world has even heard of her, or ever will. People mainly like to listen out for big blasting trumpets on television.

Marge Manoli is an old lady with a hairy mole on her cheek. She works in the Opportunity Shop on Smith Street. She calls you 'love' and she talks with you as if she really

likes you. I've heard her talking just like that to all the
crazies and all the homeless people and drug addicts who go
in there. She listens to them, even when what they're saying
doesn't make sense. She doesn't get impatient with them for
going on and on about the same thing. Marge Manoli is the
mother of Smith Street. No one ever says thank you, no one
pays her for it, and she doesn't expect anyone to either. I bet
there are millions of these kinds of people in the world –
kind, caring people disguised as bus drivers or sandwich
deliverers or mothers or plumbers.

There is Marge, and then there are all these very famous
people with more money than they need, who are famous
for the silliest thing, like being born with a big inheritance,
a newspaper, a beautiful face, or a good serve. I don't really
get that. Why should someone who is very good at hitting
a tennis ball

> backwards and forwards,
>> and backwards and forwards,
>>> again and again,
>>>> be a hero?

picture of what a tennis ball does

All those very famous, rich, powerful people just seem to
spend their time trying to get even more so – hit the ball
harder, change their nose shape so it looks better, get new

bosoms once theirs get too old, or get more money, even though they've got plenty more than they need. Now that's crazy. It leads me to think that those famous attributes must be kind of dangerous things to have. That's why I'm glad I'm not unnaturally beautiful or gifted or good at whacking a ball.

'Rich people,' I explained to Kite, thinking of Harold Barton with some alarming show of compassion, 'are crazy too. You can't blame rich people for being greedy – it's like they're on a drug. Crazy as Blue Lips. I don't know, maybe they need a lot of attention, like Barnaby. Mum was always worrying about him. She used to make him kiss her when he got home late, just so she could smell his breath, to check if he'd been drinking or smoking. Barnaby called it the kiss test.'

'Is Barnaby your brother?'

'Yep, but he went away and he hasn't come back. I know where he kept his cigarettes. I saw him get them out from his sock drawer sometimes. I had a terrapin in my sock drawer. Its name was Moby Dick, after a book that Barnaby was reading. Barnaby said it was a classic. My terrapin was also a classic. Barnaby says classics don't *do* much, they just *are*. They have a timeless quality. Moby Dick, the terrapin, was so timeless he forgot to wake up sometimes.'

terrapin inside a sock.

Kite sighed and slid his body forward onto the table and
rested his head on folded arms. He said he knew how Moby
Dick the Terrapin felt. There were days when he couldn't be
bothered waking up, either. He said he didn't like school
much and one day he was going to start a circus.

'Can I join?' I said, and he laughed. A deep river laugh.

'I'm not joking. I've been practising in trees,' I said. 'We
could go to the oval and I'll show you. Or you could teach
me something.'

Kite screwed up his nose, as if he was trying to fit the
idea in his mind, but it wasn't quite the right shape. He
started going on about how it can be dangerous and you
have to know basics first and you need a certain amount of
strength and flexibility and you need to be prepared to do
rudiments and so on. But I talked him around. I learned
how to do that from Barnaby who could talk his way in and
out of any trouble he wanted. My mum said Barnaby could
talk the legs off a wooden table. Barnaby used to start talking
to the table in the kitchen, just to show her he couldn't. But
that always made her laugh and give in. Eventually Kite
laughed and gave in, too.

'Okay, okay. I'll try showing you some basics, and if
you're good I'll train you for my circus.'

'Okay.' I stuffed my excitement down in my throat and
looked at the crumbs on the floor. There was grated
beetroot on the leg of the stool.

*    *    *

On the way to the oval, we dropped in to see Marge.

'Hello, loves,' said Marge. She was singing along to the radio. *My God is real, yes God is real,* she sang as she arranged a blue bead necklace around a foam head that was sitting on the counter. 'There, what do you think? Ooh, I like your T-shirt,' she said to Kite. 'You like music, love, do you? Do you know Mahalia Jackson? That's her on the radio.' Kite shook his head as she sang out, *Yes God is real, oh he's real in my soul . . . ooh his love for me is just like pure gold.* Marge opened her eyes wide. 'Look, love, I've got some new woollen beanies in here. Look, they're beauties.' She waddled off like a clucking chook and came back with a handful of beanies, because she knows I like them. I get them for Barnaby, too. *I can feel him in my soul,* she was singing. I tried feeling something in my soul but I wasn't sure where my soul was. I put my hand on my chest to see if it was thumping, but I couldn't be sure, so I bought an apricot beanie with two blue stripes around the edge, because it's a good cause and it only cost a dollar. I gave it to Kite, since I've got some already. He put it on, even though it wasn't that cold.

I walked along a fence wall. When I see a wall I can walk along, I have to get up on it. It's a rule. I hold out my arms like a tightrope walker. This time when I got up there I went a bit uppity, like a preacher, only I didn't go on about God and righteousness, since I know nothing about that. I just started madly casting round inside my mind for

picture of wall walking

something very important to say. Whenever I most want to
make a good impression I get like a maniac digging around
for gold. I have to sift through a lot of garbage. I open my
mouth and let words tumble out, just because I'm desperate
for some marvellous thought to surface. But it's like taking
the lid off the compost bucket and letting out all the scraps
and smells. There I was, suddenly telling how once I had a
guinea pig called John Newcombe, and then I went off on
a bee tangent. I said I like bees and Barnaby likes them too
but only because they have yellow and black stripes (which
is the same colour as his footy team, the Tigers), but I like
them because they wear pollen stockings. 'Did you ever
think,' I said, 'how a bee has a sweet part and a mean part,
a honey basket and a sting? I will probably write a theory
about that one day when I'm smart enough.'

a bee in stockings.

'Cedar, you know you're doing it wrong with your
arms?' he said.
'What do you mean?'
He leapt up onto the wall and showed me.

'When you're off-balance to one side, like this, you lean your arms towards the other side. See? That takes the weight back in towards the centre. You were doing the opposite. Like this.' He wobbled to one side.

'Oh,' I said. I stopped talking about bees then. I just shut the lid and started thinking about the circus.

✿     ✿     ✿

First thing he showed me was how to roll. We did forward and backward rolls, and sideways ones, which are called aikido rolls. They come from a martial art. He talked a lot about softening into the ground and spreading weight out like honey and making the spine long and holding tummy muscles inward and upward. When we got into headstands, he put his fingers on my tummy and said, 'Squeeze here,' but it made me laugh and I fell down.

'How do you know all this stuff?'

'My parents taught me from when I was young. They were acrobats. They were in a circus for a while, then they just had their own show which they did at festivals. I was in the act sometimes. They taught in schools, too, and I went with them to demonstrate. So I've seen them teaching and spotting kids.'

'What's spotting?'

'That's when you use your hands to support someone, so they don't get scared, and so they feel where their body is supposed to go. Like I was doing with you before.'

'Are your parents still in a circus?'

'My mum still tours around. She's a trainer with Circus Berzerkus. Do you know it? It's famous.'

'Yeah,' I lied, because I wanted him to think I'd had a life-long dream to be a circus performer. Which is just a small variation on the truth, really, since I've always been leading up to it. First, I wanted to be a vet, then a nurse, then an actress and then a gymnast, but now I've finally decided for sure. I want to be a circus performer, an acrobat.

'What about your dad?' I added quickly, to deflect any questions about Circus Berzerkus.

His head dropped.

'My dad had a fall four years ago and got a back injury, which meant he had to leave the circus. Now he works in a library.'

'Libraries are good,' I said, but I felt it was a limp thing to say, so I went up into a headstand to lift the mood.

'What's your dad do?' Kite asked me. I came down out of my headstand and lay on my back, looking up at the sky and following the clouds with my eyes.

'He died of an illness. He was a musician. But I never really met him. I was only one, when he died.'

Kite lay down, too. And for a while we both just lay like two old towels on the grass, and looked upwards. Then I told him about Barnaby. I don't know why. Probably because I blab, as Barnaby says.

✳   ✳   ✳

After the marijuana plants on the roof, Mum sent Barnaby
to a boarding school in the country. It was his final year of
school, but Mum said he needed discipline, which she
couldn't give him, and the influence of wholesome country
people, which she also couldn't give him. It really mashed up
my heart when we took him there. He had this little bed, in
a long room of little beds, that looked like a slice of toast
with a grey blanket. There were boys everywhere; a whole
bunch of them lounging on someone else's bed, laughing
and fooling around. They glanced over at us when we
walked in, and then they just kept fooling.

Barnaby sat on the bed and put his head in his hands. I
thought maybe he was going to cry. But he didn't. He just
said from inside his hands, 'Well thanks for the ride.' I think
he wanted us to go. You can feel a bit like a baby when your
family is standing over you, trying to be cheerful. So of
course I cried instead, since I'm a girl and I'm allowed.

All the way home I kept thinking about those thin beds
and him not knowing a single person – no one to even say
hi or goodnight to, or ask where the toilet is. No street to
hang out in. I wondered what he would have done after we
left – lain on the bed, crossed his legs over and looked at
that funny picture of Jesus on the wall? The Jesus had his
hands praying and he was looking upwards. On his head was
a crown of thorns that looked like flames, and you couldn't
help wondering if the Jesus thought he was going to burn.

Barnaby mustn't have liked it that much. All those

wholesome country boys and thin toast beds. After a couple of months, the school rang us and said Barnaby had run away. He called up a couple of days later from Perth! That's a hell of a long way, far across the desert. We don't even know how he got there, or what he's doing, because he must have run out of coins for the phone. Now all we get is these funny cards every once in a while.

This is a picture of Barnaby trying to do a cartwheel:

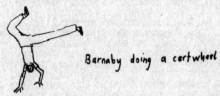

Barnaby doing a cartwheel

He's lousy at cartwheels and writing letters. But he's brilliant at cards.

Dear Mum and Cedar, in case you are wondering, here is a list of what an antelope doesn't know.

    how to tell a half-lie

    how to hold a cup politely

    how to get into debt

    when it is too late

    what is forbidden

    how to play snap

    that it is rude to stare

    that exercise is good for you

    that all antelopes die in the end.

lucky I am not yet an antelope. xxxx

'You got any brothers or sisters, Kite?' I said.

He shook his head slowly. 'Nope.' He didn't look at me. He just kept looking at the sky, and for a moment the world seemed very quiet.

☆　☆　☆

Kite said he'd meet me at the oval the next day. He didn't make a fuss about it, though. Didn't say, 'Nice to have met you, you've got potential.' Didn't pat me on the back. Just waved his hand and turned up the street. 'See ya,' he said. 'Yeah, bye,' I said, and then I walked back home with Stinky.

I often have to walk by the creek with my eyes half-closed, so that when I see all the plastic bags hooked and trapped in the trees they look like blurry white shapes. That way, I pretend they're decorative foreign birds come to visit on their way to the snowfields in Siberia. I thought about Siberia and Kite's circus. I practised cartwheels. Boy, you really should see Barnaby try a cartwheel! That makes me laugh.

birds in beanies, on their way to Siberia

Chapter 9

All day at school, I could hardly concentrate. Mrs Mayberry made me write *I must not gaze out the window* one hundred times. I'd been busy picturing myself striding past all the kids puddling around in the street. Me, looking very Lana Monroe, not even stopping to check out the street action, but moving past with animal grace, just tossing a vague look over my shoulder in Harold Barton's direction. And then I come on all Shirley Bassey and start singing in perfect confidence, *Walk on by*. My hand is twirling and I'm thinking about how I'll take Caramella Zito along with me, not that day, but when her ankle is better, and Ricci will become our manager, and Barnaby will come back to be the musical director and—

'Cedar Hartley, have you been listening?' There's the booming, irritating voice of Mrs Mayberry landing right on top of my lovely thoughts. Rats.

At home, I got all in a knot, just trying to decide what to wear to the oval. I'd never thought about it before. I even

went and looked in Mum's cupboard, but there was nothing
that fitted. I put on my blue check dress, and then I took it
off because the buttons down the front were too big and
old-fashioned, so I put on jeans with a green singlet. But I
felt a bit bare in the singlet, since my boobs just looked like
big itchy bites, so then I took off the singlet and put on a
pink T-shirt, and then I thought it would be more
interesting to put the singlet on top of the T-shirt. Then
I took off the jeans and put on an old flower-print skirt,
because my bum is really too skinny for jeans, and then
I put some grey cut-off trackies underneath the skirt, because
I would probably be hanging upside-down and I didn't want
to flash my undies. Then I put a roman sandal on one foot
and a Dunlop volley on the other, and walked about a bit
and decided that the roman sandal felt better, since I would
have to wear socks with the Dunlop, and the only clean
socks I could find had tennis stripes on them. Tennis stripes
are definitely no go. Then I went to the mirror in the hall.
I have to stand on a chair if I want to see my bottom half,
and then I can't ever get a complete effect – only one half
at a time. Boy, it's a lot of work trying to get your clothes
right. And I still wasn't sure.

clothing choices

Was it Lana Monroe? Brown eyes, chubby nose with splattering of freckles and a generous mouth. A skinny red-headed girl in a lot of clothes.

Not quite Lana, but at least I wouldn't say I'm ugly. Not that I can say I'm pretty, either. Marnie Aitkin is pretty. She has neat hair that shines in the sun. But that's not what makes her pretty. Just a lucky arrangement of eyes, nose, mouth and ears, I guess, though I don't think ears have much to do with it. Once, I went to sleep with a peg on my nose. I figured it might make my nose not so chubby, more pointed, like Marnie's. See, if braces can straighten out your teeth, then surely a peg can straighten out your nose? At least give it a dainty point. Well if it does, I swear it's not worth the pain and lack of sleep. Prettiness isn't that important. I have other winning features, like brains and high arches. (Marnie Aitkin can't jump for nuts.) Besides, there are pretty girls everywhere and I'm quite unusual, you know. Kings have married red-haired women. Not that I want to get married. I'm not even sure I want a boyfriend. Sometimes I think I do and sometimes I think I don't.

I tried a hairclip in my hair, then I took it out at the last minute, opting for the tried-and-true, low-fuss, free-flow no style. Hair out. I looked like me after all that, so I stuck my fingers in my nose — just for encouragement, and just to remind me who I was. Then I grabbed a banana, since I had no time for Weet-Bix, and off we went, Stinky and I, ready for the next training session. Potential, I said to myself.

I must have it or he wouldn't be meeting me again.

Most kids do it the other way round, but I do it this way: if I could get all the way to the oval, stepping on every crack in the pavement or line or stick or leaf or just about anything that isn't nothing, then that would mean the best possible outcome for me. That would mean that Kite and I would become famous acrobats together. But if I trod on a gap, then Kite wouldn't even show up. That was the rule.

I must have done okay with the lines. He was leaning against the pole rail with his feet crossed over. Rather casual. I wished I'd worn just trackies and not the skirt.

'Hi,' he said.

'Hi,' I said. And then he laughed, almost, and looked upwards.

＊　　＊　　＊

That was how it happened: every day after school, I went to the oval and did 'training', as Kite called it. First off, we warmed up by running around and waving our arms, then we did stretches, then headstand and handstand practice, then tumbling, cartwheeling and finally double balances. This is what double balances look like:

the candlestick

the bluebird

the flag

the fork lift          the chair          hands to feet

Caramella sometimes came and watched. Kite showed her how to spot for the double balances. Once, he tried to coax her into trying a triple balance with us, but she wedged her feet into the ground and folded her arms in alarm, saying, 'No way, I'm not going up, I'll fall.'

Kite laughed. 'You don't have to go up, you can just be a base, like this.'

He got down on his hands and knees, but still Caramella didn't want to, because she's shy and unconfident about physical things and boys make her even shyer. She wears big T-shirts, so she can hide underneath them. It's a shame, because Caramella's in the habit of covering up everything, even her talents and potential talents, but I'm working on that. After Kite left, I started teaching Caramella myself, just the simplest of things at first. It made her really happy. I could tell because she went pink and giggly and forgot to pull her T-shirt down.

What I liked best was the tumbling and the balances. I practised all the time, even at school. In maths lessons I was taking my mind through dive rolls and walkovers because

I didn't care much for maths anyway. Then at lunchtime I
went and practised in the yard, and by the time I got to the
oval after school I had already improved. Kite hardly seemed
to notice that I was getting better and better. It was as if he
just expected it. Sometimes, when we managed to hold a
balance, he'd say, 'That's good.' Never, 'Wow, you're amazing,
what potential.' Usually, he would just try to teach me how
to base the balance, but I preferred flying. He said basing was
good for building strength and understanding alignment.
Alignment of the body, let me tell you, is harder to get when
you're upside-down.

Mum even noticed something.

'So, what's going on, Cedy? Ricci says you go down the
oval after school every day. Are you getting up to mischief?'

'Nope, I swear. I'm just training.'

'What for?' She had a potato in one hand and a peeler in
the other, and she held them still as if they were waiting for
the right answer.

'The Bat Pole Championship.' I don't know why I said
that. It just came out, because sometimes you have to pretty-
up the truth for Mum; build a castle around it, or she'll
worry. Whatever I do, even if it's just lying on my bed and
imagining a tidal wave, or thinking about how I might be if
I'd been born in a faraway country like Estonia or Tuva, or
even just a town like Wagga Wagga, or even if I'd been born
as a polar bear instead of a girl in Brunswick, my mum will

immediately find a reason to worry about it. And that gives her headaches.

'What's a bat pole championship? Is it something to do with school?' she asked with a slight frown, but she went back to peeling the potato and tossing the skin in the compost bucket. A good sign.

'Not exactly, it's just a game we play, where we see who can hang upside-down for longest.'

'Oh, Cedy, you be careful. I know you. You're like a bull at a gate. You be careful you don't hurt yourself. Remember how you sprained your ankle trampolining. And then just a couple of weeks later you broke your wrist flying off that swinging rope. Well just be careful for godsake. That's all.'

For godsake herself. She's always bringing up those stupid accident incidents. Every time I walk out the door she thinks I'm going to come back limping. I'm beginning to think all her worrying about me is like some kind of jinx; she just worries so much that the world hears her and gets ideas.

The next day, it seemed like everything happened just so that Mum could say, 'Now what did I tell you?'

# Chapter 10

We started badly because Kite was late and he seemed anxious. He kept staring off into the distance and frowning. I tried to think of a joke, but all I could remember was the one about a nervous wreck and I wasn't sure it was funny enough, so I just kept quiet. He sat down for a minute with his head bent.

'Did you warm up, Cedar?'

'Kind of,' I lied again, because I didn't want to make him any more anxious.

'Shall we try the cartwheel helicopter thing then?'

'Sure.' I shrugged. We'd tried it the day before, and it was difficult. First, he cartwheels over my knees. While he's upside-down, I grab his hips and pull them in towards me. I hold on as he stands up and then I'm on his shoulders. Like this:

the helicopter

(1)    (2)    (3)

He's holding the back of my knees, and I have to arch up like I do in bird position on the pole. Like this:

(3) side view

He whirls around and I become a helicopter. He slowly bends down and puts my feet on the ground while spinning. It's brilliant — when it works.

Kite stood up with a great yawn and warmed up his arms. I did a handstand. I dropped my head and looked out past my arms. I noticed two figures standing under the willow trees. One of them waved. I stood up and turned around. Marnie Aitkin and Aileen Shelby. They walked towards us.

'What are you doing, Cedar?' said Aileen. They were both looking at Kite. And he was looking at them. Marnie was wearing one of those skirts that come down smooth and tight, and the way the sun was shining made her hair like a gold halo. She tilted her head on the side and folded her arms behind her and shaped her mouth into a secret-looking smile. Aileen pushed her hip out and opened her snake eyes, as if she'd just eaten a rabbit. Aileen had a ponytail of brown hair that she was always playing with.

'Acrobatics,' I said, tilting my head to the side, like Marnie.

'Oh really,' said Marnie. 'I love acrobatics.' She smiled at Kite and he blushed and looked down for a minute.

'Mind if we watch?' said Aileen.

Kite shrugged. 'It's okay with me,' he said, looking at me. I didn't say a word. I just nodded slightly, to show that it wasn't really okay with me, but since I'm cool I'd put up with it.

'What's your name?' Aileen said to Kite. 'I'm Aileen and this is Marnie.' She used her hand to point, just like a professional. I got this picture in my mind of Aileen as an air hostess with a navy blue blazer and very neat hair in a bun.

'I'm Kite.' He looked down at his feet and stuck his thumbs in his back pocket. Aileen and Marnie looked at each other, as if to say, 'weird name!' and then they did a small fluttering duet of giggles and shifting. Kite blushed again.

Then Marnie piped up, 'Well, do you know Circus Berzerkus? They're in town next week and we're going to see it. We're going with Harold Barton,' she added and shot a smug look at me. As if I'd care. Kite just nodded and smiled and said he'd be seeing the show, but he didn't say a thing about his mum being the trainer. Then he nodded at me and lined up for the helicopter. I stood with my legs wide and my knees bent and my mind feeling heavy and complicated like a broken-down television. I was bending low and wondering why he hadn't told me that Circus Berzerkus was coming to town, and I was annoyed and I was wishing I was pretty and going to the circus, and Kite was cartwheeling towards me, and I had to catch him, and he was pulling me

up and I was picturing Marnie at the Circus Berzerkus, and
then a sharp feeling stabbed me in my chest and I was up on
Kite's shoulders and whirling, and there were the willow
trees and Stinky and then Marnie and Aileen, snake eyes, hip
out, and the clubhouse and the willows and Marnie like a
kitten and Aileen's mouth opening, and the clubhouse,
willows, Stinky wagging, all whirling around with heads
going sideways and hips pushing out, and this pain in my
side and I was coming down and my legs went wobbly and
I sank to the ground and heard Marnie Aitkin's voice
breathing – 'Wow!'

I lay still for a moment, checking through my body bit
by bit, just to be sure where the pain was coming from. I got
up. Each time I breathed in it felt like a big spike was
poking in my side. I shrugged carelessly at Kite, as if
everything was normal, and took a careful quiet breath.

Kite looked at me, then at those girls, then back at me,
saying, 'Shall we try again? The landing wasn't so smooth.
Sorry.'

'Actually, I have to get home early, to cook dinner,' I said.
I never cook dinner.

'Can I try that?' said Marnie, hair still shining. I felt
miserable and mad. Before I had to watch myself being
replaced by Marnie Aitkin, I turned away and walked home,
without swinging my arms at all, the pain in my chest like a
fork digging in my lung with each breath. I must have
forgotten to tread on a lot of lines.

## Chapter 11

'Broken rib,' said Robert and he sniffed.

'Ah,' squawked Ricci and her mouth hung open. We were in the boys' house over the road, because Ricci had taken me there to see Robert, who's a doctor. The other boy, Pablo de la Renta, was in the kitchen cooking coconut chicken. Pablo wasn't really a boy. He was a man with hardly any hair left on his head. I don't know why Ricci calls them 'the boys' because they are both quite old, as old as my mum, but their house is much nicer than ours, although it makes you feel like you shouldn't sit down on anything in case you leave a mark. In the living room, where we were, there were paintings of lilies in Europe, and mirrors with large gold borders, and the carpet was fluffy and creamy. It made me think of England and history, but I knew it was fake, like drawings on a chocolate box.

'Nothing you can do about it, I'm afraid. Just rest and it will mend itself,' said Robert. He wasn't wearing a doctorish white coat. He had a silky lilac shirt on, half unbuttoned. He

smelled of perfume and he had hairs on the back of his
hand, but very clean nails. He smiled at me and looked sorry.
The smell of cooking chicken was creeping out from the
kitchen. It made me think of Granma, because she always
cooked chicken – not with coconut though, just with a can
of apricots and a packet of French onion soup, which she
scattered on top. I hate eating chicken, because of the bones
and the veins. They make me think of my own veins and
bones, and then I feel funny.

'She's a little daredevil,' said Ricci grabbing my shoulder.
'You be careful now.'

Pablo de la Renta came in wearing a plastic-coated apron
with little red hearts all over it. He waved a spoon in the air
and stood on his toes, and I had a horrible feeling he was
about to invite us for coconut chicken. But he didn't. He
folded his arms and tilted his head at me. 'How's the little
wounded soldier?'

'Broken rib!' screeched Ricci triumphantly.

'Oh dear,' Pablo frowned. 'Dinner's almost ready.' He
curtsied his head at Robert and then trotted out again.

'How long before it's better?' I asked.

'Probably a couple of weeks,' said Robert flicking at an
imaginary speck on his lilac shirt sleeve.

☆    ☆    ☆

I didn't tell Mum. I knew she would just say, 'Cedar, what
did I tell you?' She loves to have her worries confirmed.

It gives her more to worry about. And I didn't tell Kite, either. What would he care? I pictured him and Marnie doing bluebirds, with Aileen spotting, and that made me feel worse. Instead of going to the oval where I knew he would be waiting, I moped and wished I was there. I secretly, quietly, not-even-to-myself hoped he would be missing me and my potential. Caramella came over with some olives from their tree. They tasted awful, but Mum likes them, so I put them in the fridge for her.

'Aren't you going to training?'

'Can't, I've got a broken rib.'

'You have not.'

'I have so. Ask Robert, over the road. Ricci took me. He's a doctor.'

'Well why aren't you in hospital? Why's there no plaster?'

'I already went to hospital.' I lied for dramatic effect, since it was my only chance for sympathy. 'But they can't fix it. You can't have plaster for a rib, you just have to let it mend itself. It hurts like hell, I swear, especially when I breathe in. Don't tell my mum 'cause she won't let me do acrobatics ever again if she finds out.'

'Okay, I won't tell.'

'Promise?'

'Cross my heart and hope to die.' She licked her finger and crossed her heart, and that's something for Caramella because she's a Catholic and has to do communions with God.

✿    ✿    ✿

Caramella and I watched television. There was a man building a cabinet out of a dart board on *Better Homes and Gardens*, but it was a horrible cabinet and I said I'd rather have a dart board. Caramella agreed. So we watched *Neighbours* for a while because Caramella likes it – but I don't. All that happened was a girl was arguing with everybody and getting all steamed-up because she didn't want a traditional wedding in a church. Barnaby says *Neighbours* is monotonous crap. He likes *Seinfeld*, but I don't. I like *Great Mysteries and Myths of the Twentieth Century*. The thing I hate about *Neighbours* is that you have to watch the next one to know how it turns out, and I'm too impatient for that. I can't be bothered. I've got better things to do than care about someone's traditional wedding drama.

'Are you gonna get married, Cedar?' said Caramella, her chin bent down to her chest as she fiddled with her cross necklace, trying to make it sit the right way. Sometimes it goes back-to-front and then you can't see the little pearly roses all over it.

'How should I know?' I made out I was easy-come, easy-go by sighing a little and shrugging.

'You want to?' she said, still grappling with the necklace.

'Only if there's someone I like enough.'

'What about Harold Barton?' Caramella looked up with a broad grin. She got her cross nice and flat on her chest, and then she stroked it as if it was a cat that had just sat down. She giggled and her shoulders crept up to her ears.

'Are you crazy?' I said. 'No way. Not even if you paid me a million dollars. Harold Barton's a big ego tripper. That's what he is. *And* he pulled a swiftie on Barnaby.'

'What kind of swiftie?'

'I don't know exactly, he ratted on him or something.'

'Well, would you marry . . . ummm,' Caramella looked upward, as if asking the heavens above to offer her another likely suspect. I could tell she was about to go right through everyone in the street. Just for a laugh. But she didn't. She said, 'What about Kite?'

'Kite?' I said, and accidentally bit my lip.

'Yeah, Kite.' She fluffed up the cushion, banged it with her fist.

'He likes Marnie.'

'No, he likes you. I can tell.'

'Does not.'

'Does so. See on a daisy.' Caramella and I always did the *Loves me, Loves me not* test on a daisy. You tear off the petals one by one, and as you go you say, 'He loves me,' then, 'He loves me not.' The last petal is the final verdict.

'No, I'm not into him anyway,' I said. 'Who are *you* going to marry? Frank Somebody?' We both roared with laughter at the thought, and my broken rib hurt like mad, which made it even funnier because the more I tried not to laugh, and the more I groaned and clutched at my side, the more hilarious it got. Sometimes there's nothing as funny as laughing. It makes you feel mad, mad, mad. We got so mad

with laughing that Caramella forgot about the daisy test. She
just whacked me with the cushion. Afterwards, when she
went home, I went out and got a daisy. But I didn't do the
test. I just put it in my sock drawer where Moby Dick used
to live.

# Chapter 12

The truth is, I hadn't even kissed a boy. Once, I saw Barnaby pashing Laura Pinkstone on the couch in our living room. Normally our living room was the room where the least living went on. It should have been called the fancy-dead-room-with-dust, since no one was allowed to go in there, not unless you were a guest or the doctor. We never had guests, not proper ones, only Caramella and Ricci.

In the living room there's carpet and it's clean because no one goes in there. The couch and the chairs match. They have pink flowers and green leaves that curl all over them. I know they've been there for ages because there's a photo of Barnaby when he's just a kid and he's asleep on the pink flower couch. When Mum's not home, sometimes I go in there and lie behind the couch where there's a white rectangle of sun on the clean carpet. Through the window you can see the dusty beams of light reaching down towards you, reaching all the way from heaven or the sun or from an angel's own eyes or whatever it is that watches over us from up there. I lie in that sunny patch and it makes me go quiet and small and as still as the dried-up bugs on the windowsill. I have the feeling that time is falling on top of me, and slowly I'm getting old and still. I watch the air sparkling with falling dots of dust, and I don't think a single thought. I just let things come to me; time falling, the rays of warm air, the rumble of outside, fuzzy thoughts about dried-up bugs and vampires, and being born in Bangladesh. I can see the faded back of the pink-and-green-leaf couch where it faces the window and the sun has made it lighter than the rest. If you lift the covers on the arms (like when you pull a bandaid off a sore) you can see what the real colour was, when my mum and dad first bought it, when it was rich and tropical and everything was new and ripe, before time slowly dried everything up and quietened it down and drained out the colour and the juice . . . That's what time did to our Granma, left her with a withered and faded covering of skin, without much juice left inside. She didn't even get hungry, much, only for ice-cream with me. Especially Blue Ribbon boysenberry ripple. (Mum said Granma wasn't allowed to eat ice-cream because of her diabetes, but Granma said, 'blow that,' and she ate it anyway, on the side.) Sometimes it makes me sad to feel the way time keeps going, and you can't ever really stop anywhere, just because you like it there. Not even a couch can.

Barnaby was kissing Laura Pinkstone for a long time on the good pink-and-green-leaf couch. I know because I kept going and peeking through the gap in the door. Barnaby and Laura were squashed up on one end, and Barnaby's guitar was lying there taking up the rest of the couch. Her arm was around his back and his face was covering hers. It looked a bit boring, so I went away. But then I went and looked in again, since there was nothing on tellie. Her hand was still on his back, lying there like a lizard sunbaking on a rock, but Barnaby's hands were on a mission. One went wandering up under her T-shirt and she didn't stop him. It went up and the hand covered her boob. I got embarrassed, even though it wasn't my boob, but still.

I went and played *Can't get enough of your love babe* really loud on the CD player so they would hear it. That didn't stop them, though. I went and looked for a water pistol or a horn or something that would give them a fright and me a laugh. But I couldn't find anything. They didn't stop until they heard Mum coming home.

You can always hear Mum coming because her car makes a lot of noise. It's a Kingswood station wagon, but the K has dropped off so we call it the Ingswood. The number plate says JJH 339. That's the only line of numbers in the world that I can remember. Mum made me remember it since we always have to call the RACV when the Ingswood breaks down, and the first thing they want to know is the registration number. Anyway I like the Ingswood's number plate. It's rhythmical. When Granma was here we sometimes used to go places in the Ingswood for the whole day. When we went to Sandringham Beach, Barnaby and I could put the wave-cutter surfboards in the back and they squeaked because they were made of foam. Afterwards we had blue gelati from the van in the carpark, and they dribbled all over the seats but it didn't matter. Granma rubbed it off with a towel.

If I was ever going to kiss Kite, I didn't think I'd want to do it on the couch. I thought I'd like to do it standing up, and not for such a long time as Barnaby did with Laura Pinkstone. Sometimes I did pretend-kissing on my hand, to see what it would feel like, but I know it's not quite the same. Anyway, Kite was probably wanting to kiss Marnie Aitkin and not me, and besides, I wasn't going to think about him anyway.

But I did. I was thinking about our circus and my bung rib and that helicopter move and those girls and Circus Berzerkus and Harold Barton, though I tried very hard to think about roads and boats and being born in Bangladesh and Signor Dongato the cat. Whenever there's something on my mind and I can't get it off, I think about Signor Dongato the cat. He's just a cat from a song Barnaby and I used to sing.

*Oh Signor Dongato was a cat*
*On a high red roof Dongato sat*
*He went there to read a letter*
*Miaow Miaow Miaow*

*Where the reading light was better*
*Miaow, Miaow, Miaow*
*'Twas a love note for Dongato.*

It's the "'Twas' bit that I love to sing the best, because I do it with a certain flourish, as if I'm wearing a cape. It doesn't keep my mind happy for long, though, because I can't remember the second verse, so then I start thinking again.

I went out into the street and sat for a while on the Motts' wall, watching Harold and Frank and the others doing catamarans on the skateboards. Harold has a new fat green Golden Breed skateboard. It's brilliant, but I'd never ask him for a go. He used to have another really ace board, which was yellow with a drawing of a skull with black eye-holes on it. That yellow board disappeared and now he's got this new fat one.

'Why aren't you hanging upside-down with your boyfriend, Cedar? Did you get dropped? Got a sore head?' said Harold, and he laughed and tried a one-eighty on his board but it didn't work. He's such a spaz.

'He's not my boyfriend,' I said, and then I went back inside.

# Chapter 13

The next day there was a card from Barnaby.

dear girls, here is a fish list
golden grunter (remarkable for being able to
make grunting noise)
flathead (has a flat head)
groper (gropes)
tompot blenny (conspicuous tentacles over the eyes)
common goby (resembles sand)
spotted goby (swims through weeds in rock pool)
fifteen-spined stickleback (male turns blue when
breeding)
lumpsucker (has a worried look on face)
greater weever (anyone who gets stung while
incautiously grasping them or accidentally treading on them should seek medical attention.)
just in case you should see a greater weever please
tread and grasp carefully. I'm still by the sea but
not yet a fisherman. love B.

Obviously he was on a list trip. The card put Mum in a
good mood. She laughed when she read it. I think it was the
'dear girls'. She likes being called a girl, even though she's
really a woman. She's pretty old, actually, nearly forty, but she
looks much younger because she has a small nose. I made
the most of the good mood and dropped the big question.
I'd been warming up to it all week, slipping hints into
conversation and waiting for the right moment to go for the
kill. This was it.

'Mum, can we go see Circus Berzerkus?'

'Who?'

'You know, I told you about it last night. That
contemporary circus. Cutting edge theatre, no animals.'
Cutting edge was what they called it on the ad. It means
sharp and new.

'How much does it cost?' I knew she would ask, so I'd
rung up to find out.

'Thirty dollars, or twenty-five with a concession.'

She sighed. Her hands fluttered up to her temples and
her fingers pressed in and circled around.

'I didn't even know you liked circus.'

'I do. I'm more interested in circus than anything else.
It's the acrobatics. Please can we go? I know it's a good
circus. It isn't with animals. You'd like it, and we haven't
done anything fun for ages.'

'My god, you're as bad as your brother,' she said, because
I was talking the legs off the table. She looked out the

window at the back garden. Tin flapped on the laundry roof.
The garden looked scraggly. I know she felt tired just seeing
it. The grass was long and you could only just make out the
path where we had to walk to go to the loo. It was always
scary at night because you had bare feet and you never knew
what you might tread in. Possibly a Stinky pooh or an old
rotting bone. Mum stood up as if she was about to go out
there and stop the tin flapping on the laundry. Her arms
dropped down by her sides and then folded around her and
then she just plopped them both on my shoulders and said
I'd have to go and pick up the tickets myself since she
wouldn't have time. I said I'd do it after school.

'What about your Bat Pole Championship? Don't you do
that after school?' She was fooling. I could tell by the funny
kind of smile she had – one of those half-hidden smiles
you'd hide behind your back in your left hand, if you could.

'Oh, that. I already won the Bat Pole Championship. I
don't need to train.'

She laughed and rubbed my hair the way Barnaby does.
I always have to smooth it down again. (Barn does it because
it amuses him to watch me try to fix it up again, just so.
Mum does it because she's a mum, and mums are in the

hair before ruffle

hair after ruffle.

habit of petting and patting their kids, even though kids can grow too old for it.) I let her get away with it because I was so rapt I could hardly stay still. I went over to Caramella's to tell her.

Caramella was eating stuffed olives in front of the tellie. At our house we get in trouble for eating on the couch, but Mrs Zito didn't care. Whenever I go there she pinches me on the cheek and puts some biscotti on a plate for me. (Biscotti are Italian biscuits. They're not quite as good as squashed fly biscuits, but they're shaped like a knot, so they're tricky.)

'Guess what?'

'What?' said Caramella, who never tries to guess.

'She said yes.'

'Yes to what?'

'To Circus Berzerkus. I asked and Mum said yes. We're going. I'm so stoked.'

'Wow!' She put an olive in her mouth and nodded her head slowly. Then she chewed and seemed to be concentrating on digesting, either the olive or the fact of me going to the circus. You couldn't tell which. After a while she asked if they'd have a woman who hangs from her hair and twirls around, like she saw on tellie once.

'I don't know, probably.' I started to feel bad because Caramella wasn't coming and maybe she would have liked to. 'But maybe not, it mightn't be that good,' I said.

'Hmm,' said Caramella dubiously, and then she stared at

the tellie. It was a cooking show, with a man preparing peaches. I thought she was listening to the peach man, but she must have been thinking about things. She squinted at me. 'You should tell Kite about your rib,' she said.

'Nuh, he wouldn't care. He's got Marnie and Aileen to muck around with now.'

'You're in a huff with him, aren't you?' She had a little pile of olive pips balancing on her knees. Caramella's knees are wide and soft with a lot of flesh. Mine are knobbly and hate kneeling. Which explains why I don't go to church and Caramella does.

'No, I don't care. He can do what he likes. If he wants to hang out with them, then that's his bad luck,' I said, screwing up my nose with utmost dignity. 'Anyway, I'll probably see him at the Circus Berzerkus. His mum is the trainer, you know.'

Caramella nodded, but I could tell she had lost interest. It wasn't that she didn't care, it was just that she liked food a lot and the man on the tellie was saying how the peaches were heavenly. He reminded me of Pablo de la Renta across the road. Caramella said she preferred peaches stuffed with almonds. It crossed my mind that perhaps Italians like stuffing things. I dusted the biscotti crumbs off my lap and said I had to go. I thought I might go and tell Ricci.

'See ya,' said Caramella with the olive pips on her knees.

'Bye.'

*   *   *

'I'm going to the circus.'

'Oooooh, good for you darling. You go with that boy?'

Ricci had the hose going on the nature strip where she grows nasturtiums and lemon grass. Stinky lifted his leg on them and she shooed him off. Her hair looked funny, like hard, old cheese.

'No, I'm going with Mum. What's wrong with your hair?'

'Ah, bloody stuff. I try dye my hair from a packet. I think I leave too long. It went stupid? Bloody hell.' She pulled at bits with her hands, which made it look even funnier.

'It doesn't look bad.'

'You think? You think it's okay?'

'Yeah, at least it's not red.'

'Oh, but darling you have beautiful red hair. Beautiful colour. Oh when I was young like you, me also, I had beautiful hair. And my god I had beautiful big breasts, beautiful, you should have see. But then, oh my god, I get menopause and look—' She looked down at her boobs and put her hands underneath them. They went all the way down to her skirt. They looked like they'd be heavy, like carrying around two hotties on your front. 'Oh, it's a shame,' she said, and she tugged at her hair a bit more. I think she said that because her husband is dead.

☆   ☆   ☆

Mum said Ricci was lonely. I asked Mum if she was lonely,

too, since our dad died. She looked out the window. Her hands were holding the edge of the sink.

'Me, I don't have time to be lonely. Anyway, I've got you and Barnaby.'

'What's menopause?' She turned away from the window and started wiping the table.

'It's when you can't have children any more.'

'Have you got it?'

'Not yet.'

I checked her boobs but they seemed fine. So it's all right.

# Chapter 14

We went to Circus Berzerkus a week later. My mum was wearing her best clothes, the ones I like – the camel coat with a furry collar and the cherry-coloured skirt, and she made her hair look nice and put lipstick on. Mum looks like a rich person when she gets done up, but she hardly ever bothers. Mostly, she's the natural type. We even went to the Vegie Bar for dinner on the way. I had a tofu wrap and she had Singapore noodles, and the waiter called us ladies. I had my green beanie on and Mum didn't even complain about it. She was just cracking jokes about how I should have worn the tea cosy instead. We caught the tram into the city. In my mind I was trying out opening phrases that I could say to Kite when I bumped into him.

*So, what's new?*

*Hi, how's it going?*

*Well whattya know?*

*Kite, hi, remember me?*

Or to be really hip . . . *Dude! So how's the helicopter going?*

No, no, much too fake. Not at all me. I would never say that, and if I tried it would be obvious that I was trying.

I couldn't find one that seemed right. My brain was skittering with excitement. Excitement makes me jiggly – in my mind and in my legs.

'Cedy, you're jiggling,' said Mum. So I crossed my legs underneath me.

*     *     *

The circus was brilliant, except for the juggling, which went on a bit. I don't like it when they juggle knives because I get worried. It's like horror movies. I can't watch them. My hand flies up and covers my eyes whenever there's murder or gory stuff. The best bit was when these people dressed in white came flying down from the roof. They were attached to strings and they just swallow-dived down like a flock of great white birds. Mum liked the tightrope walker, because he got dressed on the tightrope and ate cornflakes, and went to work. Everyone laughed at him except me. I never laugh when I'm supposed to. I only laugh by accident. In the interval we could see Harold Barton with Marnie Aitkin; they went outside and smoked cigarettes but we didn't say hello. Mum bought me a Choc Top. I looked about for Kite.

'You looking for someone?' said Mum.

'No, just looking at the people.'

'You've got chocolate on your nose.' She giggled at me, and swiped at my nose with her thumb. I hate it when she does that. I ducked because I like to get my own mess off myself, thank you very much.

'Wanna bite?'

'No thanks.' My mum prefers a cup of coffee to a Choc Top. She's crazy like that.

✿    ✿    ✿

After the circus finished, Mum saw her good friend, Maya, who has red hair like me and works at the environmental farm by the Merri Creek. I still hadn't seen Kite. I didn't care. Yes I did. I was wishing I had seen him and I was trying hard not to care and to think instead about what a good circus it was but I was getting all mixed-up in my mind, and fidgety. Mum was talking to Maya about a festival to celebrate the return of the kingfisher to the creek. I was only half-listening, just standing there going up and down on my toes and waiting for Mum to finish, when I got a kick up the bum. I turned around.

It was Kite. He was with a tall guy who looked mental.

'So, what happened to you? I thought we were training.' I could tell he was cross. His arms were folded. The mental guy was smiling.

'Well, I thought you were training with Marnie.'

'Why'd you think that?'

'I dunno, just did.' I felt stupid all of a sudden. I'd been acting like a schmuck. Maybe it was only my crazy over-active imagination that had decided it was on with Kite and

Marnie? I tried to cover it up with a good, slightly true excuse. 'Anyway, I couldn't come. I broke my rib doing that helicopter. The doctor said I had to rest it for two weeks.'

'Bull,' he said, and shifted his weight from one leg to the other. 'You're making excuses.'

'No I'm not. It's fair dinkum. I promise. Cross my heart,' I said, just as my mum turned around. I thought I was a goner, but she mustn't have heard me. She smiled at the tall guy as if she knew him.

'Hello, Oscar,' she said. 'Did you enjoy the show?'

'Well yes, it was quite good I thought, quite elaborate.' He kind of spat the words out, and he wobbled.

'Yes, you're right,' said Mum. 'It was elaborate.' Then she turned to me. 'Do you two know each other?'

'No, I know Kite.' I introduced my mum to Kite, and then I met Oscar and then we all stood there a bit awkwardly since no one knew what to say, until Oscar pointed at me.

'You've got something on your nose,' he said.

'Chocolate,' I said, rubbing it off. Mum smirked because I hadn't let her rub it with her thumb, and Kite let a small smile creep out, even though he was annoyed at me. But then, since I was now clearly the overall loser with a kind of pie-in-the-face smear of Choc Top on my nose, I took advantage of my underdog rights to plead for another chance. I asked him if we could start training again the next day.

'No, I can't tomorrow. Anyway what about your rib?'

'It's better.'

He looked at me the way he does sometimes, as if he can see inside. He laughed and turned to go. Then he hung his head down for a bit and did a neat little spin on his toes back towards me.

'What about Saturday?'

'Okay,' I said a little too quickly. He raised his eyebrows in a slow way, as if they were heavy, or as if he was lifting his gaze upwards in order to see over the top of my eagerness. I quickly looked down at the floor and drew an invisible line with my foot.

'So you wanna come backstage and meet my mum before you go?'

'Can we?' I looked at Mum.

'I'll wait here, love. You go. Just don't be long.' Boy she was in a good mood. She didn't even ask about the rib till later on, and when I said, 'Oh just a bruise,' she nodded sympathetically.

I didn't stay long. Backstage was just like it is in the movies. Mirrors with light globes around the edge, and people with white faces and bunches of flowers, hugging and shouting and rushing about. Kite's mum was leaning up against the bench, talking to a man who was sitting at the bench and taking off his white face. He was looking into the mirror and she was talking and smoking and looking straight ahead, or up towards a corner, but not at him either. She wore black pants and she had straight black hair hanging to her shoulders. She seemed very shiny and compact and well designed, like a box that expensive jewellery might come in. When she saw Kite she took his face in her hands and stared at him. Then she kissed his forehead and said, 'Hello my darling.' But she didn't hug him.

Kite introduced me and Oscar and she smiled over the tip of her nose at us saying, 'Pleasure to meet you.' She was all straight lines and tips and angles. She asked Kite if he liked the show and what did he think of the tumbling sequence with the hoops and what did he think of the trapeze and did he like the music. Her eyes were very insistent. They seemed to be digging inside and searching about for something that was lost. She didn't ask Kite how school was. She said, 'And how is your father? Didn't he come?' Kite said his father was okay, but he didn't want to come to the circus. 'How's his back?' said the mother. Kite shrugged and said it was just the same. And then neither of them said anything for a while, but she smoked quite ferociously on her cigarette and looked out her eyes sideways. She called out to a woman, 'Shirley, come and meet my son.' Then she grabbed Kite by the hand and dragged him around, showing him to the people in the circus. I think she forgot that Oscar and I were there.

Oscar leaned up against the wall and said, in his slow stumbling voice, 'Well she isn't a pussy footer is she?'

'No she isn't,' I said, and giggled because Oscar made

a funny face and I liked him for wobbling there with his wide face. The whole dressing room was full of people who were like lights blinking on and off in bright colours, except perhaps for Oscar who, in the midst of all that flashing, seemed suddenly stable and good, like a familiar lampshade with a warm unremarkable glow and a couple of sore spots and no reason to try to be brilliant or celebrated or better than the rest. I would have liked to stay and lean against the wall with him in a quiet colourless way, but I thought I'd better go.

Oscar said, 'Well, it was nice to meet you.'

'Likewise,' I said, and then I ducked out the door.

We went home on the tram. I told Mum about Kite and she told me about Oscar. He's one of her clients. That means he's an accident victim and she helps him with things. She's called a carer.

'What happened to him?'

'He had some kind of fall so he's got a slight brain injury, which is why he sounds funny when he talks and why he wobbles a bit on his legs.' She said there's absolutely nothing wrong with his mind and that he isn't at all mental, and that his mind is actually very original and sharp and imaginative. There's just a slow connection in the motor part of his voice.

'I wonder how he knows Kite,' I said.

'Yes, I wonder.'

# Chapter 15

Mum read the card from Barnaby out aloud at dinner.

Imagine you are walking around and around.
Perhaps you are in a city or a forest or in a room
full of excited people... As you walk you notice the
sound of a crowd murmuring, the sound of a man
treading over leaves, someone's perfume stings your
eyes, a woman with a bandaid across her chin asks
you for a cigarette... all this happens and more.
I remember how the old couch groans a little when
you move.
love and groaning from Barnaby.

'Oh, that boy. He gets it from your father,' said my mum,
shaking her head as if she disapproved, but I could tell she
didn't really disapprove, she just worried. She stuck the card
on the fridge with all the other ones.

'Gets what?'

'Oh, you know, this crazy card thing. It's just like

something your father would have done. Barnaby's off in his own world. We can't even contact him. And he knows how I worry.' She was tired. There was a dirty mark on her shirt. She was licking her finger and wiping at it but it wasn't going to go, I could tell.

'Was our father like that?' I said, pushing my peas under the mash potato. I didn't mind peas so much, but that's what Barnaby always did with his peas. Mum leant her head in her hands. She looked at me like I was an innocent child, even though she knew I was half grown-up and had once hit a man on the head with a kumquat I lobbed from the hedge.

Now she just rested her eyes on me and said softly that my father just had a very lively imagination, he was a dreamer, and had I finished my dinner, and was I going to please stop playing with the potato and start eating it? Conversations about our dad were always closed before you could really open them. It bugged me. Trying to talk about our dad was like walking up a very short dead-end street.

✻    ✳    ✶

'Mum, what illness did our dad die of?'

'It was just a sudden thing.'

'Was it cancer?'

'No.' Her fingers started tapping on the table.

'Mumps?'

'No.'

'Diabetes?'

'No, that's what Granma had.' Her hand went flat and still for a moment.

'Myxomatosis?'

'No, that's only for rabbits.'

'Heart attack, then?'

'Oh Cedy, yes, I suppose it was a kind of heart attack. Haven't you got homework?' She stood up and her chair screeched on the floor as it moved.

'I did it already. Mum, don't only old people die of heart attacks?'

'Usually. It depends. Sometimes you ask too much of your heart and it can't take it. You can wear it out early.'

'Is that what our dad did?'

'I s'pose so. You shouldn't think about it.' She sighed and started fussing around the kitchen.

'Mum, did you cry when our dad died?'

'Yes, I did.' She didn't look at me. Her hand went to her mouth.

✿　✿　✿

There's this ad on tellie where a girl's crying because she's in trouble at school and then her dad comes to get her. He's wearing a suit, he's handsome in an old Sean Connery kind of a way, and I can tell he would smell nice. He sorts out the trouble. When the daughter sees him she's happy and you can tell she feels safe. The father hugs her and takes her schoolbag and opens the car door for her. He has a much

better car than the Ingswood, one that would never break
down. I bet she doesn't even know the number plate. The ad
is stupid. I can't even remember what it's advertising. I get
the feeling that there's something fishy about my dad dying,
but no one will tell me what.

✳   ✳   ✳

I went and lay on the old couch and tried listening to it
groan as I moved. It doesn't really groan, it yelps and puffs.
Barnaby exaggerates. I wanted to ask Mum if she thought
Barnaby was asking too much of his heart, too, but I didn't
because my questions make her tired. So I did a headstand
and checked to see if my rib hurt, but it was okay. I was
ready, for Saturday.

    I remembered how, not long before Barnaby went,
Mr Barton had come over. You could tell he was foaming
at the bit about something, and I hadn't thrown one single
kumquat near him. You could tell by the way he banged on
the door – bang bang bang, not knock knock knock. His
face was all squeezed-up and his hands were pushing hard in
his pockets, like they wanted to jump out and smack you but
they weren't allowed because he's a dad and he wears a suit.
Mum took him into the living room and closed the door,
and they talked too quietly for me to hear. That time I think
it was something to do with Barnaby.

# Chapter 16

I should have known. Kite should have known, too. You'd
have to be thick not to know that between the months of
May and September, nearly every oval in Victoria is taken up
with footy on Saturday. There were people all round the
edge of the oval, watching. It was only boys playing, but still,
boys and their parents get very serious about footy. I only
like it when someone gets a mark way up high, by jumping
up on someone else's back and snatching the ball out of the
air miles above everyone. That's what I'd do.

'Well, we can't train here,' I said. Kite and I were sitting
on the rail and looking at the match.

'Nuh, doesn't matter, we can go to my place. We've got
mats there.' His hands were balled-up and stuck under his
T-shirt. He twisted his head sideways to look at me. But I
wasn't giving anything away. I just gave a breezy shrug.

'Can Stinky come?'

'Course. Dad would like to see him again.'

'Okay, let's go then.' I jumped down off the rail. Kite had

asked me to his place – that meant we had to be friends. I
didn't care about mats or no mats. I felt like swinging my
arms around and hooting, but of course I didn't. I stood
firmly on my buzzing feet and smiled. Kite slid off the rail
and shoved his hands in his pockets, and looked up at the
sky as if something was about to fall out of it.

✿    ✿    ✿

I met his dad. They lived in a small house with a long hall
and windows on only one side. So it was dark, and smelt like
wet socks and bathmats. The other side was joined to
another house that looked almost the same. It wasn't as
messy as you might think a house without a mother in it
might be, but it wasn't swept and stainless and steely, like the
Bartons', and there were no good cooking smells like at
Caramella's. Also, there weren't any pictures on the walls or
things on shelves, like at our house. It was a house without
things. At least without little things. For me, since I'm a
major snoop, it was a bit like opening a photo album and
finding it empty. Kite's dad was sitting at the kitchen table
reading the newspaper, just like my mum does on Saturday.
She reads the Extra and sometimes cuts the Leunig out and
sticks it on the fridge. Kite's fridge was bare.

Kite's dad stood up when we came into the kitchen. Kite
put his hand on the back of my shoulder and said, 'This is
Cedar.' The hand stayed on my shoulder for quite a few
seconds. I could feel it. And when it left, there was still a

warm feeling where it had been. The dad shook my hand and smiled and said, 'Nice to meet you. I hear you're a great acrobat,' which made me go red and protest that I wasn't, even though secretly I knew I wasn't bad for a beginner. He was wearing trackie dacks and his hair was all ruffled-up, as if he'd just got up. He picked Stinky up and tickled him under the chin. His eyes were like washed-out rain clouds – big and sad and pale.

'We're going to do some training in the garage,' said Kite.

'Good on you,' said his dad. He nodded encouragingly, and smiled, and seemed a bit shy, even. But I thought he was nicer than the mother. He seemed soft, like flannel pyjamas. 'Can I look in?' he said, and he put Stinky back down.

'Nuh, not yet. Maybe later,' said Kite. The dad nodded. He folded his arms and held on to them. He seemed not to know what to do, even though he was the dad and we were only the kids.

'Oscar dropped over before. I told him you wouldn't be back till this arvo.'

'Thanks. I'll go over later.' Kite opened the fridge, looked in and closed it again. 'Do you want a glass of water?' he said to me, and you could tell the dad felt bad because there was no cordial or juice. He started saying he'd go and buy some apple juice but Kite told him not to worry.

I said, 'I like water and we only have water at home too because Mum says cordial makes you hyperactive and I'm active enough as it is.'

I think the dad appreciated me saying that, because he laughed.

*     *     *

We went out the back, which was mainly cement with a Hills Hoist and some building rubbish in the corner. I asked Kite about Oscar, but he didn't really reply. He just pointed to the garage at the end of the yard, and said, 'Check it out.'

Garages have never appealed to me. Attics do and gardens do, but garages are usually full of men's things that smell bad and have sharp, heavy edges that rip your dress or hurt if you drop them. I struggled to get excited by the appearance of two brick walls with a roll-a-door mouth.

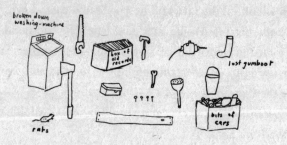

*broken down washing-machine*

*box of old records*

*lost gumboot*

*rats*

*bits of cars*

*things you find in a garage*

But inside it was another story. This garage wasn't made of black corners and greasy holes. There were no cars, tools, or petrol stains. And no calendars with pictures of Hawaiian women in bikinis. It didn't look at all like a garage.

Firstly, there was a patch of dirty cream carpet on the floor and a window with sun coming in. The walls were painted blue and there was a big stack of foam mats in the corner. Hanging from the ceiling was a trapeze which was tied up so you couldn't reach it. There was a ghetto-blaster in the corner and a few pictures stuck on one wall. I felt like a kid in a new playground.

'Wow, some garage!'

'Yeah, my folks used it for training. When they were together.' Kite was flinging the mats on the floor and fitting them together like a jigsaw. I looked up close at the pictures. Some were photocopies from *The Tumbler's Manual*, by Laporte and Renner, which Kite had already told me about. There were drawings of a short man with no face, in speedos, doing companion balances with another exactly-the-same man. Pretty advanced stuff, like high arm-to-arm balances, hand-to-foot pitch somersaults, ankle-toss flying back rolls, knee-and-shoulder springs, neck-lift back somersaults. There were dots to show you the movement pathways. Like this:

diagram of knee-and-shoulder spring

'Can we do this one?' I said pointing to the knee-and-shoulder spring. I felt sure we could do that. Almost sure.

'Maybe. We'd need Dad to spot it first.'

There was also a picture of his mum and dad when they were younger. The black-haired mother was standing on the dad's shoulders, wearing a white disco suit with sequins. They were both smiling hard. There was another one with Kite in it. It was a large black-and-white photo of all three standing on their heads, laughing. Underneath was the same shot, only they weren't laughing and their legs were in tricky positions.

'Why didn't your dad go to see Circus Berzerkus with you?' I asked.

Kite flopped on his tummy on the mats. 'I dunno. I think it makes him sad. 'Cause he's not in it any more. And he doesn't like to see Mum, anyway.'

'Why not?' (Barnaby would say, at this point, I was being nosy.)

'Oh, she's got a boyfriend in the circus. After Dad had his accident, my mum went off with a man called Howard. He's the music director in the circus. So Dad lost a lot all at once and it makes him feel bad to see it. It reminds him. I don't think he likes his job in the library. He's stuck looking after me, and Mum goes around the world with the circus and Howard.' Kite rolled on his back and squeezed his knees up to his chest, taking a deep breath in. 'We don't like Howard much, Dad and I. Dad calls him The Weasel. Mum rang that day. Remember the day when you broke your rib? They had a big fight on the phone. I listened to it. They always fight. Dad told Mum to just bugger off out of his life. He told her

she was selfish and she didn't care about anyone but herself.
I heard him say it.'

That explained Kite's weird mood that bad Marnie-and-
Aileen-bung-rib day. I went and leant on his knees; it helps
the stretch. I was looking directly down at his face. It looked
back up at me blankly.

'Do you like your mum?' I asked.

He turned his face away. 'I dunno.
Aren't you gonna start warming up?'

*a good stretch*

'Yeah.' I lay on my back like he was.

'Do you like yours?' he said, looking straight up at the
roof. His voice came out with a stumble, as if it was running
over rocks.

'My mum? Nuh not much. Sometimes she makes me
mad.' I don't know why I said that. It wasn't true. Well in
some sense it was true. I felt mad at her for always rushing
and always being too tired and never being home after
school. But then if I didn't like her I'd be glad she wasn't
home. So I must like her. And if she had a heart attack, like
Dad did, or ran off with a circus, I would feel really rotten.
I'd feel like those people felt when the *Titanic* was sinking
and they knew they had to jump into the ocean all on their
own. Well maybe not quite that rotten, but almost. It hurt
a bit just to imagine my mum not being there, so I didn't.
So I did a back roll because I'm impatient and I'm also a
show-off. Kite wasn't watching, anyway. He was still staring
up towards the ceiling. Probably thinking about his mum.

# Chapter 17

The thing about boys is that they don't talk in the same way as girls. They talk about things. Out-and-about things, things you can touch and see, not the kind of things that are inside. Those inside things aren't really things at all, since you can't see them – not with your eyes – and you can't hold them – not with your hands. So they're situations. I call them situations of the heart. Boys don't talk about heart situations. If they're blokish, they talk about bulky things that move, like cars, footballs and chicks. If they're natty sharp, they go on about plug-and-socket things, like computers, stereos and science experiments. I think really smart boys probably talk about the government and the theatre, but there aren't many that smart. The smooth talkers talk about girls they see on the tram, and older boys like Barnaby talk about music, bands and marijuana, and what an antelope doesn't know. I don't think many boys talk about what an antelope doesn't know; only Barnaby, because he's a dreamer like our dad was.

It's not that girls' talk is better or more important, not in subject matter anyway, because honestly some of them only talk about boys and how to make boys like them. That's the older ones, and it's so boring. I wouldn't do that because I'm a feminist and I plan to get my own opinions about the state of the world and I wouldn't ever let a boy tell me how to get them or what to do with them, either. It's the *way* girls talk that's different. With girls you can go on and on about tiny little things that happen to you. You're allowed to take an hour to tell about an argument you had with your mum, and how it made you mad or sad or both. You can't do that with boys.

Kite hardly ever talks about those inside things. Like when he told me about his mum and dad, he just said it as if he was talking at the roof and not as if he was sharing something with me. And when you ask him personal questions, like about his friendship with Oscar, he kind of blocks them, or fobs them off or swipes them away as if they're flies bothering him. That's kind of what Barnaby does, too. Not Caramella, though. She wants to chew the fat, as my Uncle John would say. That means you linger on details, you chomp right through the facts and get to the bone, the nitty gritty gristly chewy sense of things, the gooey core, the centre of that messy weave of feelings that bury into your skin and wrap you up. Not that you can ever hit that centre, but if you hover around it for a while you can get some kind of blurry view of it.

When I got home from training with Kite at his house, Caramella wanted to hear everything. I know Caramella is my friend, because when we talk it makes me feel that what I felt and saw and said in any kind of situation means something.

'What was he wearing?'

'Just the same kind of thing he always wears. I don't think he thinks about it.'

'Did you ask him about the tall guy at the circus?'

'Oscar. Yeah, I asked but he didn't really answer me. I don't think he wanted to talk about it.'

'Hmm. That's funny. What was his dad like?'

'He was nice. There was no cordial. He was going to go and buy some. Actually, I think he was sad.'

'How could you tell he was sad?'

'Just could. He had a sad look, and he spoke quietly, like a kid who's shy. Anyway, Kite said he was. Because Kite's mum left him and now she's with a man called Howard who's like a weasel and Kite's dad has to work in a library.'

'Oh, that's bad.' Caramella bit at her nail and frowned and considered the situation. Then she said, 'What kind of house do they live in?'

'A small one. It's dark, but out the back there's this ace garage with mats. That's where we train.'

'Was Kite pleased that you wanted to keep training?'

'I dunno. He didn't say. You know what he's like, he doesn't say how he feels.'

'Well, couldn't you tell?' (It becomes a girl's job to read a boy's unexpressed feelings in other ways. Girls get good at looking for signs.)

'No. Maybe.'

'Did you get that funny feeling?' (The funny feeling is when you like someone and your tummy goes all empty and pounding and words bury down blunt inside and suddenly erupt out your mouth all wrong, like a spew, so you go red in the face, because it matters a great deal that you make a good impression.)

'At first I did, but after a while I felt normal.'

'So, you've got a crush on him, haven't you?'

'He put his hand on my shoulder,' I said, faintly sidestepping the question, because I wanted to draw it out, make it last, like eating an ice-cream slowly.

'How long did he leave his hand on your shoulder?' said Caramella.

'For a while. I felt it go through me.'

'You have got a crush. I can tell.' She folded her arms triumphantly, as if she'd just won a game of Fish.

⁺    *    *

I went home and thought about whether I had a crush or not. I only wanted to have one if he had one, otherwise it would be awful. There was a card from Barnaby.

*Do you ever worry that your skin might wear out*
*if you keep washing it or burning it in the sun*

like it was toast, or padding your feet up and
down the road and bending over, making tired
creases in certain places? What's inside your skin
making you walk on and on?
Oh the deep air and the song it surrenders.
Although I am a superb singer the birds are better.
The air would be empty without them. I am afloat.
A black swan stole my heart. I am a wandering
whistling duck in love with a black swan.

swan     and     whistling duck

Sometimes Barnaby can say things in a sideways way. I
used to go and bug him after dinner, when he was meant to
be doing homework but never was. He was just sitting on
his bed playing guitar.

'Barn, do you love Laura Pinkstone?'

'Nuh.'

'Then why were you kissing her on the couch in the
living room?'

'Well. I guess I loved her when I was kissing her.'

'But not afterwards?'

'Well, not all the time.'

'So, sometimes you love her, and sometimes you don't?'

'Yeah. One third of the time I love her but two thirds I
don't.'

'How can you tell how many thirds?'

He put his guitar down and leaned close.

'Cedy, I may be wrong, but the way I see it, there's three parts to love. Three ways of doing it – mind, body and soul. When you get all three happening at once, that's it. That's the real thing.'

'Which part is it with Laura?'

'Body.'

'Oh.' I frowned because that seemed to me to be the dodgiest part. Not that I know. I only know what you see in the movies and sex always leads to trouble.

'Look, Cedy, Laura's nice. I like her, but hey, (at this point he opens both his hands and grimaces) she doesn't get it. She thinks straight up and down, she can't go round corners. And I myself like to bend the view a bit. That's all.'

'Have you ever had all three parts going on at once?'

'Not yet. Have you?' He smiled.

'Get real.' I screwed up my chubby nose and gave him a punch. Barnaby started singing *Love Serenade*, and I pondered the three-part theory. After a while I decided that love shouldn't have anything to do with maths and parts. I told Barnaby, and he said, 'You're right, it shouldn't. Love and maths, they're in a different ball park.' Then he started singing it, *Love and maths, they're in a different ball park*.

And I think *I'm* exasperating!

✿    ✿    ✿

When Mum got home I showed her the card from Barnaby.

'Do you think he's really in love?' I said.

She laughed. 'I hope not. He might never come home if he is.' She sat down on the couch, took off her shoes and started rubbing her foot.

'Mum?'

'Yes.'

'How did you know when you were in love with Dad?' I took her foot and started squeezing it for her. She loves it when I do that. She lay her head back on the armrest and heaved a big, long sigh.

'You can just tell, by the way you feel, I guess.'

'How did you feel?' I wondered if it was the funny feeling, if that was love.

'Well, you feel like you want to be close to that person, you feel happy when you're with them, or you do at first.'

'Then what?'

'Well, it's different for everybody. With your father and me, love got complicated by other things.'

'What other things?'

'Oh, just life, you know, dirty dishes, different dreams. Why the questions, Cedy? Are you in love already?'

'No, course not. Barnaby said there were three parts to love.'

'Did he? Oooh, that's good (referring to my thumb action on the sole of her foot). You'll have to do the other foot now or I'll feel lopsided. One foot will be envious of the other.' We swapped the feet over.

'Barnaby said there's three parts to love: mind, body and soul,' I said, not letting up. She smiled, but she didn't reply, not straightaway.

'Soul, that's the main one,' she said. Then she closed her eyes.

# Chapter 18

'I heard you whacking last night. Was it the rat?' said my
mother at breakfast. We have to eat brekkie quickly, because
she drops me at the tram stop on her way to work and we're
always running late. I got out the Vegemite and spread it on
cold raw bread, because I didn't have time to toast it.

'Aren't you having butter?' said my mother.

'No, the butter's too hard. It only works on toast. It
makes the bread rip.' Mum only has coffee for breakfast, so
she doesn't understand the fine art of toast and spreading.
She won't buy margarine either. Always just hard unsalted
butter.

'You were whacking the wall at two o'clock in the
morning.'

'Yeah, it was the rat again. It woke me up.' The rat lives in
the walls of our weatherboard house. It's a big mother. I can
tell by the noise it makes, especially when it decides to do
major nest renovations right in the wall next to my bed. It
wakes me up. I used to throw shoes and books at the wall,

but now I just whack it with Barnaby's old cricket bat,
which I keep by the bed. That night, I whacked like crazy
since I was particularly annoyed at the rat for waking me up
from a good dream. In the dream I was on a mountain and
there were animals lying down and Barnaby was there and
we were climbing up, because our father was at the top
waiting for us, and then I saw Kite and he gave me some
chewing gum which made me feel dizzy, and then scratch,
scratch, scratch went the blasted dream-disturber rat. So I
never got up the mountain to see my father, but that's how
it always goes in dreams – you never get where you really
want to go.

   Mum said it's the chooks that attracted the rats and the
mice. Barnaby brought them home from the Vic Market for
Mum's birthday. So, since it was a birthday present, she had
to be grateful and keep them, even though I don't think she
really wanted them. They live in the backyard. I named them
Rita Hayworth and Door. Rita Hayworth is red but she
doesn't sing. Door is a follower – you know, like a door –
just getting pushed around, open and shut. Not much
personality, but lays a lot of eggs. Whereas Rita Hayworth,
she squawks and looks awfully good. I like naming things.
Sometimes I walk along the street, naming all the little bugs
that live in the holes in fences and on leaves and the middle
of flowers.

*     *     *

'I'm seeing Oscar today,' said Mum. We were in the
Ingswood on the way to the tram stop. I was eating my
bread and Vegemite in the car. I told Mum to say hi from
me. Then I remembered that Oscar was in my dream; he was
on the mountain eating a boiled egg and I said I'd bring him
back another one, but I got distracted by the sleeping
animals and wanted to lie down, too.

I dug into my school bag and grabbed a pen and bit of
paper and wrote a quick note.

> Hi Oscar, do you like eggs? We have two hens.
> My brother is a whistling wandering duck and
> I am learning to fly. from Cedar.

I gave it to Mum to pass on to Oscar. I didn't even care
if she read it.

birds in various positions

# Chapter 19

'Cedar, get down!' Kite yelled and grabbed my ankles. I was just swinging a bit from the trapeze, like this:

*flying position*

He had gone into the house to get some water. While he was gone, I just thought I'd try out a bat position on the trapeze. And then I just let it swing a bit. And then I let it swing out even more. And then I felt my body sailing through the air, all the bones loose and free, and it wasn't me doing it, it was another force, a force that lay and waited in the air and caught up birds and balls and falling leaves and everything that falls and flies. It made me feel I was knowing something special, at least until Kite came and yelled at me and stopped the swinging.

'I can't get down while you're holding my ankles,' I said. He let go and helped me down, even though I didn't need him to. His face was white and angry.

'What's wrong?' I said.

'Are you stupid? Don't *ever* hang upside-down without mats underneath. And even then, don't do it all on your own. You haven't learnt yet, about safety. It's really dangerous if you fall like that.'

I'd never seen him angry before. He was almost yelling and his hands were making jerking movements in the air, like Mr Zito when he's mad at Mrs Zito.

'Okay, okay. I won't,' I said, but I felt a bit huffy or funny or battered so I went and sat down. For a horrible moment I thought I was about to cry. I turned and faced the wall just in case. He didn't say anything, and it seemed to go on like that for ages with me just sitting, facing away from him biting back tears, and him just standing there being silent and angry. I didn't know how to stop it. I thought I might just leave but I couldn't. I couldn't picture it working right. He'd think I was a big sook.

'Cedar, shall we try the flag?' He sighed and put his hand on my shoulder again, in just the same place, only this time he squeezed it a little.

'Okay.' I turned around.

'Sorry for yelling,' he said and grinned. I nodded, but I didn't quite let a smile out. Not right away. I had to warm up to it.

This is what the flag balance
looks like when you get it right:

This is what it looked like
when we did it:

Sometimes we do it easily, but I was flustered and forgot
the right grip and kept falling off. I was getting discouraged
and annoyed and about ready to throw a tantrum, so I gave
up.

'Hey, Kite, do you wanna just go walk through the Motts'
hedge instead?' I said. After all, I was truly tired, because of
the rat-induced sleep deprivation. Too tired for concentrating
on what grip for what balance.

'Sure.' He did a head-flip and landed on his feet. 'Enough
training, let's go.'

✿   ✿   ✿

The Motts' hedge is long and bushy at the top, like used
paintbrushes. It runs between the Motts' house and the
Bartons'. Once you get up at the level where the branches
fork out, you can travel along all the way from one end to
the other, hidden on the inside in a tunnel of trees. The thing
is you've got to walk, not climb or clamber like the little
kids do. You have to walk with the same assurance that Jesus
must have had when he was showing all the disbelievers that

he could walk on water. You have to try to stay straight-up, and without looking to find places for your foot to go. You get lots of scratches, but it's worth it. To walk through trees, makes you feel brilliant, like a super hero. Once, Hoody Mott jumped out of the hedge for a dare, but he broke an ankle, so now we're not allowed to jump.

Kite was better at hedge-walking than anyone. I knew he would be. When he went up the tree he went all monkey. He seemed to know just where to reach, where to lean out, when to make a little jump. And he seemed to know it without thinking, as if his body knew it.

'You're like a monkey,' I said. We were at the end, where Hoody had jumped. We sat up high in the hedge, dangled our legs down and looked out at the street.

'Yeah, when you climb you think monkey, when you run you go panther, when you fly you become bird. It's a trick my dad showed me.'

'Whaddya mean?'

'Well, the body thinks faster than the mind. And it doesn't think in words. It's no point *telling* your body what to do, but if you put an image in there, an image it can *feel*, then it can use it. Like, if you want to jump really high, you imagine yourself having springs inside you, you imagine your chest is being pulled upwards by a rope, you imagine your arms are reaching to catch hold of a balloon high up in the sky. That's how my dad teaches me things. He makes me imagine. Dad reckons you could fly if you could feel it right.'

'If you become bird?'

'Yeah. See, that's why he called me Kite, after a bird, so I might fly.'

'Does he want you to fly?'

'Not until I'm ready.'

'Are you ready yet?'

'Nuh, not yet.'

'Do you wanna fly?'

'Course I do. That's what I'm gonna do. Don't you want to?'

'No,' I said. But I was just saying no because I wasn't sure I'd ever be able to anyway. For now, I told myself, a good back-flip out of a round-off would be enough of a flying kick for me.

I pulled a seed ball off the branch and let it drop. We watched it plonk on the ground and roll a bit. The time I got Harold's dad with a kumquat from up in that hedge, he freaked out a bit, and pounded on our door like a bear with a sore head. I watched him from the hedge. Barnaby said Mr Barton deserved a kumquat in the head because he was having a love affair with Mrs Mott, and everyone knew except Mr Mott, who was a slowpoke. Mum said you shouldn't listen to idle gossip, and Mr Mott wasn't a slowpoke. He just wasn't a match for Mrs Mott, and whatever the case, I had no right to kumquat Mr Barton. She grounded me for two weeks.

*   *   *

From up where we were in the hedge we could see Pablo de la Renta in his front garden, snipping at roses. He had his plastic-coated apron with hearts on. I yelled out hello and he stood on his toes, flapped his secateurs at me and asked how my rib was. 'Much better,' I said. Pablo de la Renta had a roly-poly melody in his voice; it broke out like waves.

'Don't fall from the tree,' he said, and he frowned like a mother would, and bent back over his roses.

'Who's that?' said Kite.

'He's one of the boys. The other one, Robert, is a doctor. They live together in that white house there. They have very, very posh furniture, and a banana tree and sundeck out the back, and Mum says they complain about our chooks because the chooks attract mice, and they complain about Ricci feeding the birds because the birds poop on their cars. But otherwise they're okay.'

'And what's going on over there?' Kite pointed down the street. It was Harold Barton, and sitting in the gutter nearby were Hailey and Jean-Pierre. They were just watching. Hailey was holding a rabbit. Harold had a bit of metal. He was jamming it into the manhole on the road and trying to lever the lid off. Barnaby said that Hoody Mott had opened the manhole once with just his little finger in the hole, but I don't know if that's true. If you looked through the hole you couldn't see anything, but you could feel a wet-dirt smell coming up and hitting you in the eye.

When he got the lid off, Harold went and came back

with a big, dark, heavy object. I couldn't tell what it was. He put it in the hole and then he put the lid back on.

I called out, 'Sprung, bad Harold, we saw you!'

'Saw what?' said Harold, squinting upwards. I wished I had a kumquat to drop on him. 'Well, look, it's young No-hoper Hartley.'

'What was that you put in the hole?'

'That's for me to know and you to find out.'

'Whose is it?'

'Wouldn't you like to know.' He used his sneery voice and put his hands on his hips as if he was the boss. Jean-Pierre yelled, 'Car's coming!' and everyone got off the road. Harold gave me the finger and ran inside. I looked for something to chuck at the car. Another seed pod, that was the thing. If a car came by and you were in the hedge, you *had* to throw something. That's how I got Mr Barton with the kumquat, right through the car window. Bull's Eye.

'Let's go see what he put in that hole,' Kite said, and then he jumped, from exactly the same place as Hoody Mott. He didn't even check or consider, he just sprang outwards, opened his arms wide and pressed his chest upward. I swear, for a moment I thought he was about to fly over the whole street. But he didn't. He dropped and landed on the Motts' lawn, folding at the knees. He looked back up over his shoulder at me. 'Think bird,' he called up. But no way was I going to jump. I'm not that stupid. I climbed down.

'You're mad to do that. I know a guy who broke his ankle jumping from there.'

''Cause he didn't land properly, that's all. It's not that high.'

Hailey came up, still holding the rabbit. She looked at Kite as if he was Superman, as if she was checking to see if he was real.

'Did you hurt yourself? Hoody Mott broke his ankle. We drew flames on the plaster.'

'Nuh. I'm fine. What's your rabbit called?'

'Madge.' Madge had grey ears. Kite patted Madge and then he jerked his head towards the manhole. 'Let's go check it out.' I knew Hailey and Jean-Pierre would be envious of me because I was hanging out with the guy who could jump out of a hedge better than Hoody Mott. I tried not to gloat, not on the outside. I gave them an obliging look which said, 'You can come too.'

Kite lay on the road and put his eye on that small hole in the lid. It's a round, heavy lid made of steel or iron or something, so that cars can drive over it or you can jump on it as hard as you like and it won't bust. There's a hole the size of a twenty-cent piece right in the middle.

'Can't really see it,' he said. The stolen thing.

'Nuh, I know, it's too dark in there.'

'I know what it is. In the hole. I saw,' said Jean-Pierre, rushing over all importantly. He had a cashew-coloured tummy which stuck out a bit over his shorts. His hair was

very short and stood on end like a nail brush, which always
made him look a little alarmed or electric. I bet he still
sucked his thumb at night.

'What?'

'It's a light. Like a lantern. They all stole it. Patrick
and Harold and Frank, from Hutton Street. Where the
roadworks are. It's to stop the cars driving into the big
hole in the road at night. They're gonna get in big trouble
if someone catches them. What if someone drives their car
into the hole?' Jean-Pierre shook his head and his mouth
made an O shape, and you had the feeling he wanted to
see someone get in big trouble. But he wasn't going to
be the dobber.

'Why's Harold putting it in the hole?'

Jean-Pierre shrugged. 'Dunno. Just to hide it.'

I was a bit envious, actually. Harold having a hidden
thing in that hole. Once, Barnaby put a whole lot of water
in it, but that wasn't any good – you have to put something
that needs hiding away. A stolen thing is the best. Something
that someone is looking for. That's what makes it thrilling.
There can't be hiding if there isn't seeking; it wouldn't make
sense. Like if no one is looking for you, then it's boring to
hide. Even Stinky knows that. He only wants bones and
sticks if you pretend *you* want them, and chase him. Hailey
asked us if we wanted to go to her house and see where
Madge the rabbit lived, but I said no thanks. Hailey always
wants to play blackboard games, and she gets huffy if you

don't play it her way. She sulks off when you start adding ears or roots or revolting words to her drawing.

✿    ✿    ✿

Kite and I went to my place to watch tellie. Ricci was walking back from the boys' house with her little puffy dog, Bambi. She moaned and said Bambi wasn't well, but then she smiled and showed us her fancy new grey-and-orange slip-on sneakers that she got from the Chinese two-dollar shop. She said Prince William had the same ones. She saw a picture of him, in a *Women's Weekly*. She laughed and said Prince William must be bloody cheap like her – they only cost five bucks.

# Chapter 20

Usually I didn't ask people over to our house, not kids
from school, because at other kids' houses there would be
a mother there to make sure you weren't going to burn
the house down, or drink the Bailey's Irish Cream, or get
kidnapped by a boogie man. Also, the house would be
much tidier than ours, and there would be stuff to eat,
like squashed fly biscuits or icy poles or red cordial.

Once, Tophy Sutton from school came over and when
she saw in our cupboard she said, 'boring, boring, boring'.
She said our stuff looked like jars full of bird food. Then she
told everyone at school the next day: Cedar's mother eats
bird food, Cedar's mum works, Cedar doesn't have a dad.
Tophy Sutton said that because she lisps, and she likes to
point out other people's shortcomings, too, just so that she's
not the only one with stuff that makes you different and
good for a stir. I didn't get her back, like I could have. I
didn't say one thingle lisp joke. Tophy's real name is Sophie
Sutton. For a while she got called Thophy Thutton, but then
she told Mrs Mayberry, so we shortened it to Tophy.

Our cupboard has a lot of things like lentils, rice and sesame seeds. Mum says people call it bird food because they don't understand nutrition. Still, I'd be happy if we had squashed fly biscuits. I gave Kite a Granny Smith and a handful of almonds, because it tastes good if you put apple and almond in your mouth at once.

With Kite, I didn't care about our big messy old empty-afternoon house, because he didn't have a mother at home, either, and his house was untidy, and he didn't even have cordial. We sat at the kitchen table and I showed him the cards from Barnaby. They're all stuck on the fridge with magnets.

'He's loopy,' said Kite.

'Yeah. He makes you laugh.'

'Why did he leave?'

'He ran away from boarding school because the beds were thin.'

'When is he coming back?'

'We don't know. He doesn't leave an address. We don't even know where he really is, except that it's Perth somewhere.'

'Do you miss him?'

I stuffed a big handful of almonds in my mouth. I had to think about it. I never would've thought that I'd miss Barnaby, because we used to have some big barneys. Once, he punched me in my mouth because I kicked his sandcastle, and I got a chipped front tooth. But that was when we were just kids, and now that he's seventeen he never punches me. And he doesn't kick me out of his room, either. He lets me sit on his bed and ask questions. Mostly, what I missed was just him being there, even if we aren't in the same room talking. I missed all the stuff that comes along with him: his weird singing, the trouble he gets into, the things he knows. I like that. I liked it when the family felt bigger, with Granma and Barnaby. Four of us was enough to feel like a regular family. Now there's only two, it feels too small to be a real family. It feels like a thing with holes in it. So, did I miss him?

'Yeah, kind of. It's quiet here now,' I said. 'Wanna watch tellie?'

*    *    *

We sat on the couch. Stinky got up with us, even though he's not allowed. It was nice just sitting on the couch and watching tellie. We weren't even talking, and we weren't sitting so close that we were touching. It would be funny to touch on a couch, even though when we're practising balances we hold wrist-to-wrist, or stand on thighs, or grab hips. I even sit with my boney bum on his feet, like this:

the chair

But it's not the same if you touch on a couch. On a couch it would *mean* something. Just before he left, Kite dropped his hand on my leg and leant towards me.

'Hey, I better go. Mum and Howard are taking me out for dinner before they leave again on tour.' He took his hand away and stood up. So I stood up and walked with him to the door, like my mum does when she has guests.

'Where will you go for dinner?'

'Somewhere fancy with white table cloths. I don't really want to go, not with Howard, but I have to because I won't see my mum again for a long time.'

'Do you miss her?'

'I'm used to it now.' He kicked a stone and it went hurtling off and crashed into the fence.

'Well, seeya tomorrow?' I said.

'I can't train tomorrow, I'm busy.' He looked down and put one foot on top of the other.

'Okay.' I looked at his sneakers. They were dirty and old.

'So I'll see you Wednesday?' he said.

'Okay.' I wanted to ask him what it was he had to do, but I didn't. I could tell it was secret. Of course, after he went I thought about it and I was sure he was going on a date with Marnie Aitkin. They were going to Luna Park or the movies or even a fancy restaurant with waiters in bow ties, and she would be wearing some kind of sexy necklace, and he would notice it and she would giggle into her hand with the coral fingernails and—

*Oh, Signor Dongato was a cat.*
*On a high red roof Dongato sat,*
*Oh Signor wrote a lady cat, who was fluffy white and*
*nice and fat . . .*

☆    ☆    ☆

I went upstairs and tried on some of Mum's lipstick, but I don't think it made me pretty. I tried talking at the mirror with the lipstick on. I tilted my head sideways like Marnie does. Then I went and tried watching tellie with it on. Just to get used to it. Mum came home.

'You look glamorous,' she said.

I rubbed it off with the side of my hand because I felt stupid.

'Look, I got Ratsack,' she said.

'What for?'

'To get rid of the rat. I can't have it waking us up every night.'

'You're going to poison it, not get rid of it.' Grown-ups can be so sneaky with words, you have to watch out for it. 'You can't poison it. What about animal rights?'

'Cedar, it's vermin!' Vermin, another one of those camouflage words that are used to justify the slaughter of little critters.

'It's an animal, a mother with babies.'

'Oh, stop it Cedar, you're being silly. Look, Oscar gave me a note for you.'

A distraction device. I took it and shut up about the rat.
For the time being.

dear cedar, yes I particularly like scrambled eggs
on toast on Sundays. With peas. Tommorow However, I
shall be attempting to cook a splendid cake with about
six eggs in it. If you are hungry please come and try
it after school. Number 59 Hickford St. we have no
hens or whistling ducks but there is a stuffed donkey
and a picture of Indian cricket players. Love Oscar

Lucky I wasn't training, after all. I love cake.

# Chapter 21

Oscar was mowing his front lawn when I arrived. He was wearing a red cape tied around his head, a bit like a shepherd or a wise man in biblical drawings. It billowed out behind him. He stumbled forward on the grass behind the mower. I yelled out hi. He turned off the lawnmower and raised his hands in the air, his face like a child who had just seen something exciting, like a cow, out of the car window.

'Oh, I'm all right,' he said grabbing my hand. (He must have thought I said, 'how are you?') 'I'm trying to be useful, come in.' He took me inside and introduced me to his mother.

Oscar's mother was very old, and very tall like Oscar. It didn't suit her to be so tall. She was very talkative and she hunched her shoulders forward, as if she mightn't otherwise fit inside the house. She said the house was in a terrible mess and her husband should have done the vacuuming, since he's been laid-off work, and would I like a drink of lime cordial. Oscar's father was at the pub. The house looked completely in order and arranged to me, plus there was a mother and a father not far away, and cordial. I was impressed.

For a minute I thought she was about to ask me questions about my family, but she didn't, luckily. She just squeezed out a smile and went and poured the cordial.

'Oscar's made a cake.'

I wasn't sure what I was meant to say, so I just smiled and looked at my hands. There was dirt under my fingernails. Oscar laughed into his lime cordial and it spluttered everywhere. The mother frowned, and said, 'Oscar why don't you show Cedar your books?' I was wishing I'd washed my hands. They're always grubby from handstanding on the street. I can walk around on my hands for about twenty-two steps. Oscar started to say something, his voice rumbling and stumbling. The doorbell buzzed right on top of the rumbling voice. Oscar's mum was wiping up the lime cordial. Oscar lumbered and lurched towards the door.

'Kite's here,' he said, words ejected like bullets. Then he smiled at me. 'It's my birthday.'

Kite was wearing the apricot beanie. I went red. He looked surprised to see me. I don't know why, but I felt as if I'd just been caught doing something wrong. Oscar's mum talked loudly, wiping her hands on a tea towel.

'Hello, Kite. Would you like a lime cordial? Oscar's made a cake. It's chocolate and orange. You know Cedar, don't you?'

'Yep, hi Cedar. I didn't know you were coming.' He raised

his eyebrows at me. I didn't think he looked thrilled or out of his mind with happiness to see me. He seemed even a bit suspicious. Then he gave Oscar something that was wrapped up in newspaper. 'Happy birthday, mate,' he said.

Oscar sunk into a chair with a big gasp. He unwrapped the present very carefully and slowly, as if the wrapping paper was the kind that you might have to keep and use again. (Mum always makes us use things again.) But it was only newspaper. If it was me I'd have ripped it off, but then I have no patience. It was a book, a small hardback. *Drawings and Observations* by Louise Bourgeois.

Inside, there were almost abstract drawings with a paragraph of writing. The drawings were kind of unusual; wobbly, funny, awkward and confusing. But Oscar loved it. He beamed and stood up and threw his arms around Kite, nearly whacking him in the nose. Oscar's mum brought the cake over and we sang happy birthday. Oscar wanted to know where Kite found the book and Kite said he went and looked around at the Art Bookshop and of all the books this was the one that reminded him most of Oscar's books. So I asked about Oscar's books, and Oscar's mum said Oscar was an artist of sorts. Oscar laughed and said he was just doing the only thing he could, and would I like to see?

Oscar's room had a single bed with a blue cover, and a large desk with a muddle of pens and paints and jars and paper and books. All over the walls there were pictures stuck up with Blu-Tack; some were photocopies of old diagrams, some were drawings, some were photos of stars or pyramids or colour pages ripped out of a book. There was a photo of Oscar riding a bike with his hands off, the way Jean-Pierre does. He looked different – brighter and strong. Oscar shoved a black hardcover book into my hand saying, 'Here, look, this is mine.' Kite picked up some socks and started juggling them. I sat on the bed and looked at the book. The first page was just a word written in shaky writing. It said *Commonplaces*. The rest of the book was full of pages and pages of drawings with words, like this:

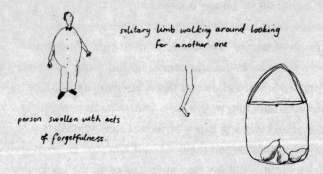

solitary limb walking around looking for another one

person swollen with acts of forgetfulness.

green pears in your bag getting little brown bruises on the way home.

I liked it, but I can't say why. Perhaps because it was odd and small and quiet, not grand, and because it made you smile just a little inward smile, and the way it scratched at your mind, like a funny tickle. Not a big one. It wasn't big, but still it made you wonder. It made you think maybe you were a solitary leg wandering around looking for another.

I told Oscar that I liked it and that my brother would too. Oscar was sitting in a chair and letting his arm dangle down. He said again that it was all he could do. Then he dropped his hand on his knee and his eyes went sad.

'I've got a brain injury,' he said, his hand thumping up and down, stuttering on the knee. He turned just his eyes towards me, head bent forward, his smile like wire stretched taut across his face, eyes like dark windows on a limousine, the bright look that I saw in the photo gone dim, as if it was covered in shadow. Somewhere behind those eyes, I thought, there was a part of Oscar all locked up. I wanted to say something, but I couldn't think what. I looked at Kite, who had his hand on Oscar's shoulder. He'd hardly said a word to me all afternoon. I said I had to go. Oscar said he was happy that I'd come and please come again and look at all his other books. He said it seriously, with a slow purposeful weight, as if he was lowering a precious piece of furniture to the ground, and then he pointed to a stack of black books on his shelf. I went and said goodbye to the mother.

'Thank you for coming, Cedar. Oscar rarely meets new friends now. He'll be so pleased you came.' I asked how long Oscar had known Kite. She seemed surprised.

'Hasn't Kite told you about Oscar?'

'No.'

'Oscar's our youngest, you know. His brother and sister have left home.'

'Oh,' I said, hoping she would say more.

'Kite and Oscar were best friends when they were just kids. They used to ride around together on bikes. They used to do a lot of things. Kite was learning acrobatics from his father, you know. The mother was never there. Oscar took an interest. Those days, Oscar took an interest in anything.'

She broke off and a cloudy look came over her face. I tried to picture Oscar running and riding skateboards and climbing trees and shouting. She started talking again.

'I don't know what they did together in that garage, how far Oscar got with the acrobatics, but anyway, one day Oscar took it upon himself to practise hanging upside-down on the Hills Hoist out the back here, and he fell. He was alone.' She sighed and twisted the tea towel in her hands. I almost could have guessed what she was going to say. 'He landed on concrete on his head. That's how he got the brain injury. He's all right now, he loves his art work. But you know, Kite is about the only friend of his who has stuck by him. The poor dear felt terribly responsible for Oscar's accident. But of course Kite couldn't have known Oscar would try out things on his own. In some ways, Kite took it worse than Oscar, I think. He's very protective with Oscar. He won't let people make fun of him. Of course, Oscar's getting better all the time. We hope he'll just keep improving.'

'Yes, of course. I hope so too,' I said, and my mother would have been proud.

*     *     *

That explained why Kite got so angry with me for hanging on the trapeze. It made me think about how Mum always worries at me too, and how I always get annoyed at her worrying, because she's just such a big worrywart, and why can't she see that I'm well co-ordinated? I know I go around as if I'm some kind of Bionic Woman, like I'm invincible. But of course I know that I'm not. No one is. Not even Barnaby. After all, I really did break a rib. So no wonder Mum worries. I wish she wouldn't.

I leapt up on the wall and walked along it, thoughtfully and carefully.

'Why do you always walk on the wall, Cedar? You look like a dag.'

Aileen was standing beneath me. Next to her, surprise surprise, Marnie Aitkin. I stayed where I was on the wall. They seemed smaller that way. Marnie's mouth was half open, as if her jaw had just got too heavy to close. I looked firmly into the small snake eyes of Aileen.

'I walk on the wall because there are snakes all over the pavement.'

'Oh sure, very funny,' said Marnie with relentless predictability. Then she folded her arms on her chest, rolled her eyes and shook her head at me. I didn't think she looked very pretty. I kept walking. *Think Dinosaur* I said to myself, and I became larger and larger.

'Hey, Cedar,' called out Aileen. 'We want to ask Kite to a party. Can you give us his number?'

'Haven't got it. Sorry,' I said, without even turning back, because luckily, as I said, the only number I know is the Ingswood's number plate, JJH 339. That's the truth.

'Liar,' one of them called out, but I didn't even look back to see who.

☆    ☆    ☆

When I got home from Oscar's, I went outside to put Rita and Door in the chook shed and I saw Madge the rabbit, chomping on the long grass. I got Hailey and Jean-Pierre and we chased Madge around the garden until Hailey caught her.

'Madge keeps getting out. We're moving to our Grannie's house,' said Hailey.

'Why?'

'Because we have to. Daddy says.'

'When?'

'Next week.' Madge weed on Hailey's leg and she said 'Yuk' and went home to wash it off.

✳    ✳    ✳

Ricci came over with a dish of capsicums stuffed with cheese and rice and herbs.

'Here, darling,' she said plonking them on the stove and then grabbing the Wettex to give the stove a vigorous wipe. 'I make too much for me.'

'Hailey's moving,' I said.

'I know.' (Of course she knew. You can never tell Ricci something because she always knows first.) 'They were evicted.' She said that just to prove she knew more than me, and then she slumped down at our kitchen table and started to moan.

'What's wrong, Ricci?'

'Oh darling, my dog, Bambi, he need an operation, but the *bloody* vet, he wants me to pay 500 dollars. Oh you think I have that much money? Of course not. I ask my cousin to lend me money and she say no. Ooh she a miser. I very unhappy. I take my Valium, but I still unhappy. You know how much I love my dog.' It was true. She loved her little fluffy yapping Bambi as if it was her baby. I was worried.

✿    ✿    ✿

Mum came home, grinning.

'What's so funny?' She started to laugh.

'I just saw something funny.' She raised her eyebrows and poked her finger at the capsicums. 'Did Ricci bring these?'

'Yep. What did you see?'

'Mr Abutala. You know, Hailey's dad?'

'The fat man?'

'Large, not fat. Yes, him. He was shooing this rabbit into the Zitos' garden, with a stick.'

'That's Madge. That's Hailey's rabbit. It was in our garden before.' Mum giggled and put the capsicums in the oven.

'Well, looks like maybe Madge isn't wanted round at their house, and Mr Abutala is trying to find Madge a new home. Let's hope Madge doesn't get into the boys' garden, or Pablo might make a stew out of her. Did you thank Ricci for the capsicums?'

'Yes. And I gave her some eggs. What does evicted mean?'

'Why, who's been evicted?' She looked worried.

'They have, the Lebbos.'

'Cedar, don't call them that. Evicted means the landlord has told them to leave the house. Do we want a salad?' She opened the fridge and squatted down to look for lettuce.

'Can we be evicted?'

'Anyone who rents a house can be. It doesn't mean they did anything wrong. Sometimes the people who own the house just want it back.'

I didn't like the idea. I'd got used to this old house and this street and the way you can go to the creek or to Smith Street. One thing I can't stand is how you never know when someone or something is going to go away. Now I couldn't even be sure our house was going to always be our house. And then what if we had to move out and Barnaby wouldn't know where we were. 'We'd lose Barnaby if *we* were evicted,' I said to Mum. She was washing the lettuce in the sink. She sighed a big sigh, because she worries about Barnaby, and I can tell she misses him because sometimes she goes into his room and just sits there. She said she was sure we weren't about to be evicted yet, and Barnaby would come home soon, and could I check the capsicums in the oven. I told Mum about Ricci and her dog. Mum said she would definitely lend Ricci the money if she could but she couldn't – not all of it, but some, perhaps.

After dinner I went to my room and got an idea. I always get ideas when I need them, especially if I lie still and think.

# Chapter 23

Kite and I were doing dive rolls through a hoop, taking turns to hold the hoop.

'You weren't very friendly yesterday at Oscar's,' I said.

'Sorry,' said Kite and he smiled.

I did a big dive. I love dive rolls.

'You can go higher. Don't hold your breath,' he said.

'Why weren't you?'

'Why wasn't I what?'

'Friendly.'

'I don't know.'

'Because of Oscar? Because you thought I might make fun of him?'

'Yeah probably. He cops a lot you know. Kids think he's a mental.'

'I don't think that. I like Oscar.'

'Well, I'm sorry, I just didn't know.'

'That's okay. Can you hold the hoop higher then?'

✳   ✳   ✳

After training, we were in his kitchen eating cornflakes with honey. He kept smiling at me. He had a spoon in his mouth but still he kept smiling.

'What?' I said.

'Nothing.'

'You keep smiling.'

'Do I?'

'Yep.'

'It's because *you* do.'

'Do I?'

'Yep. I—' He stopped with his mouth open, then he closed it again and looked down at his cornflakes. 'I dunno, I like training, that's all.'

I don't know why, but it made me feel the funny feeling when he said that. So I flicked a cornflake across the table and quickly changed the subject before I started blushing or something. I told him my new idea. First I explained about Ricci and her dog who needed an operation. Then I said it.

'I thought we could do a circus show, to raise money.'

'You and me?'

'Yep, you, me, maybe Oscar could do something. And Caramella. Whoever. It would be like a benefit. For Ricci's dog.'

'We'd need a lot of people to come.'

'Yep, but that just depends on advertising. We'll ring up the tellie and put an ad on there.'

'Where would we do it?'
'Here.'
'I'll have to ask Dad.'
'Yeah. Ask him tonight.'

Chapter 24

There's a long way between an idea and a real thing. Inside
your mind there is a boundless view. You can imagine
whatever you want. For example, you can plan exactly how
you would like your house to be; you close your eyes and
picture spiral staircases with slippery banisters and blue
wooden floors and stars stuck on the ceilings and a grass
carpet for rabbits in the rabbit room and sometimes there
might be a white cow on the couch or a herd of wild
wandering albatrosses, wearing new hats and recently
returned all the way from Russia to tell you tales, waiting in
your bathtub which is as big as a bus and always perfectly
warm with honey-scented bubbles. And through the
diamond shapes on the windows, all you can see is every
kind of tree, even mountain ash, and some with swinging
ropes and the warbling of lemon-bellied fly-catchers and
laughing kookaburras and some festooned with rare spotted
birds that sing like Stevie Wonder. And then, just at the
moment when you're in the trees swinging from a rope and

going all Tarzan, your mum yells out and you have to open your eyes. '*Cedar! dinner's ready.*'

So you open them, and lo and behold, there you are just lying on your back facing the cracked ceiling above you, which is blotchy with dirty yellow puddles as if someone peed on it. That's how it really is. Real life is a bit like a used tea towel. And you can't get even one single albatross to wear a hat and tell you tales in the bath, no matter what you do. Some ideas just have to remain as ideas.

In my mind I went to town on the circus idea. I mean I really went mad. I lay on my bed and I couldn't stop imagining it, bigger and bigger, all cutting edge of course, and theatrical and magnificent, with dramatic lighting and a live band with cymbals clashing at every spectacular moment. Me, riding a galloping white horse, in fact doing a handstand on its back, looking oh so Lana Monroe in a costume which glitters, and with feathers in my hair. Then from the roof comes Kite, swooping down, (either he's flying or he's attached to a rope, looking excellent in his camel corduroys and a beanie) and the cymbals are clashing and trumpets blasting and lights flashing as he grabs me by my ankles and the audience goes *oooh!* as we swoop up and up and the show begins . . . Only I forgot, there are no animals.

And it's in the garage.

And I'm not really sure if Kite can fly or not.

✿    ✿    ✿

'Did you hear me, Cedar? I said dinner's ready.' Mum wasn't in a good mood. I could tell by her tired voice. And earlier, when she got home, she had listened to the messages on the answering machine and then she sat down and cried. I heard her. She didn't know I was home, because I was in my room being quiet and ant-like, concentrating with unwavering determination on circus ideas. I rolled off my bed in the way that all acrobats naturally would. When I walked into the kitchen, Mum wiped her eyes quickly and stood up and pretended she was looking out the window, out onto the weedy yellowed garden. She said something about the chooks, Rita and Door, just to make it convincing. But I knew.

'Are you okay, Mum?'

'Yes, I'm fine, just had a hard day at work.'

'What happened?'

'Oh, I had a difficult client. A couple actually. I had to take Matteo – you know the old Italian man who still thinks he is twenty-two – I had to take him to McDonald's. He wears a very nice suit. It was alcohol that did it to him. He lives in a home and this is his outing for the day. He's difficult, because he doesn't know how old he is. So he sits in the car and he puts his hand on my leg or round my neck and he says, 'I love you, I love you.'

My mum does this very well. She acts it out, putting her mouth close to my ear and crooning in an Italian accent, 'I love you, I love you.' I laugh and she laughs.

'What else?' I say, because I know sometimes she needs
to talk about the things that happen to her at work.

'Oh, apart from two long and tedious hours of playing
Snap with Joy, the worst part of the day was Renata. I was
teaching her to cook. We made biscuits and I said she
should share them with everyone at the home she lives in.
She refused. She said only if they came to her one by one
and asked. Then she might give them just one, but only
if she liked them. It wasn't fair. The ingredients belonged
to everyone at the home and, anyway, she has to learn not
to be so selfish. No one likes her. I insisted she share them,
and she threw a plate at me and called me a bitch. I left.
I'm not going to work with her again. She's too
volatile.'

'What's volatile?'

'Unpredictable, explosive, like a volcano, about to go off
any minute. Like Pablo de la Renta on a bad day.'

'Oh,' I said, thinking that could be a good name for our
show.

'Did you hear the phone messages?' said Mum, who was
picking at her food but not really eating it.

'No, why, was there one for me?'

'There's one from Barnaby, I think. You listen.'

*   *   *

I dropped my fork and went to listen. It was just guitar, with
a little breezy humming. No message. Definitely Barnaby. I

smiled but I felt mad. He could have said something. I wish
he'd say something. He sounded like a far-off wind.

'That's him, for sure,' I said.

She nodded and smiled and her eyes went soft. 'Funny,
when I first heard it, I thought it was your father.' She
looked away from me. I thought she'd gone mad. My father
was dead and couldn't leave a message even if he wanted to.
Then she sniffed and shrugged. 'I mean, of course I knew it
couldn't be, but when you want to you can almost fool
yourself.'

I frowned at her. Had she really lost it?

She patted my wrist. 'Your father used to play and sing
down the phone at me when we were young, just like that.
And Barnaby sounds so much like him.'

I nodded. Not because I knew that, just because I
understood. I understood why she had come home and
cried. It wasn't really work and Renata throwing the plate, it
was Barnaby's message. It was my dad not being here any
more. Being dead.

'Maybe it means Barn's coming home soon, Mum?' I said.

'I hope so.' She looked all funny and sad again, so I
changed the subject.

'Guess what? Me and Kite are going to do a circus show,
as a benefit, for Ricci's Bambi.'

'Kite and I,' she said. (She can't help correcting me,
because she's a mother. They get used to looking out for
what you're doing wrong, instead of what you're doing right.)

'Kite and I are doing a circus show,' I repeated slowly. She smiled and seemed half worried. She said would I please be careful and were we using anything high and was anyone helping us? I lied and said Kite's dad was helping us, and then she felt better about it.

'Have you told Ricci?' she said.

'No, it's a surprise. You know, just in case it doesn't work out.'

✿    ✿    ✿

Kite and I started the next day. Kite had a whole lot of ideas, too. We spent the afternoon jumping about from one idea to another. He'd say, 'Let's try this,' and we'd do it for a bit until I'd say, 'I've got a better idea, why don't we do it this way?' And then he wouldn't like it that way for one reason or another (like he'd say it was daggy or overdone or predictable) and so we'd start with another thing altogether, until we both got sick of it. So we stopped and went inside for some cornflakes, and we sat there at the table and we didn't speak or smile at all. Then I said, 'Maybe if Oscar and Caramella came and helped, it would be easier?'

He slumped forward on the table and, knocking over his bowl of cornflakes with his elbow, said that would make it worse and we had to work out first what we wanted them to do, and Oscar couldn't balance properly anyway, and Caramella was unco. We got in a bit of an argument about Oscar and Caramella, because I thought it would be a good

way for them to be a part of something. Kite said it might
make them feel bad if they couldn't do things well, and I
said it wouldn't matter, we could find a thing they could do
well, something they're good at, not necessarily acrobatics.
He sighed and I felt bad. There was a puddle of spilt milk
trickling towards the edge of the table. I put my finger in it
and drew a square. Maybe Kite was right. It was too hard.
Kite's dad came in.

'What's up? How's the show going?' He put his hand on
Kite's slumping back.

'We didn't get anywhere,' said Kite without even looking
up.

'Ah,' he said. And immediately I felt better, because he
said 'Ah' the way a doctor does when he understands what's
wrong. 'Too many cooks, I imagine?'

Kite screwed up his nose and nodded. I wiped up the
milk. Kite's dad sat down and smiled. I was hoping he might
offer to help, but he didn't. He asked me if I'd had a drink
(lately he'd been buying apple juice) and he looked sadly at
Kite who just slumped there. He tapped the table with his
fingers and it made an annoying sound. I felt like frowning,
because of the annoying sound and the milk and Kite
slumping. But I didn't. I just stared out the window. I didn't
know what to say. Half of me just wanted to give up on
the whole thing. But half of me didn't. The half of me
that wanted to give up was the bad half, the sooky half that
wanted everything to be easy; that half just wanted to go and

flop on my bed with Stinky and stare mournfully at the blotchy ceiling. The other half kept imagining how it could work, if we wrote a plan, or took it in turns to be the boss, if we just kept trying.

'Do you reckon you can help us, Dad?' Kite looked up slowly. He was squinting, as if the idea was being squeezed out his eyes, as if it was hard to ask. His dad seemed relieved. He stopped tapping and he slapped his hands down happily on the table.

'I'd like to give it a try.' He looked at me. 'What do you think, Cedar? Are you willing to let an old guy have a go at directing your show?'

'Sure.' I didn't give it a second thought. That was the firmest thing I'd ever heard Kite's dad say, and his eyes opened wide and bright. I suddenly felt light and good and excited. I could almost have gone and started again right then.

'Okay, we'll start tomorrow,' he said, and even he seemed happy. Kite gave me a wink. I tried to wink back but I'm a hopeless winker; both my eyes go at the same time, like a blink. He laughed.

'Lucky your handstands are better than your winks,' he said.

# Chapter 25

Kite went to see Oscar, and I went straight over to
Caramella's to ask her if she'd join our circus. Stinky weed
on their silverbeet, but Mrs Zito didn't see and I didn't tell.
Mrs Zito gave me a pomegranate off their tree. Caramella
and I went and sat on the Motts' wall and shared the
pomegranate.

'Guess what?' I said, spitting out a pip as far as I could.
(The pips are covered in a soft blood-red jelly which you
suck off.)

'What?' Caramella never guesses.

'We're starting our own circus.'

'You and Kite?' she said, dusting her round knees and
bending her head.

I got another pip on the tip of my tongue, and curled my
tongue to make a kind of wind tunnel, and then I blew
hard. The idea was to get the pip onto the road. Caramella
didn't even look up to see where it landed. She sighed.

'We want you to join. Will you?' I said, nudging up

against her. She still didn't look at me. Her head was droopy.
Her hands were clasped together and the thumbs were
wriggling. I heard her sniff a big breath in. It wasn't how I'd
expected. I thought she'd be rapt.

'No. I'm not good enough. You know I'm not.' She
sounded far away, as if she was buried underneath her own
skin. I tried to look her in the eyes, but she wouldn't look at
me.

I told her she was good enough and I wouldn't have
asked her if I didn't want her in it. I put my arm around her.
She still looked down. I enthused some more.

'I want you for all the Caramella kind of things you can
do.' I said. 'It won't all be high balances, it'll be low ones,
too. Anyway, it's not what you do, it's how you do it, even if
it's just walking or standing or speaking. It's about *performing*,
Caramella, because whatever you do, you'll do it in your
own Caramella way, no one else's way, and that's what we
want.' I was getting confused. I thought I knew what I
wanted, but I was only just working it out as I said it.

Caramella sniffed. 'Does Kite want me in it too?' Her
thumbs stood still, like little exclamation marks. It occurred
to me then that perhaps Caramella had been feeling left out.
Lately I'd been spending more time with Kite, and that
meant less time with Caramella. She was still my best friend.
I was just temporarily distracted. But it's terrible to feel
forgotten, even if you aren't really.

'Yep. Look, right now Kite is asking Oscar to join, too.

Oscar doesn't do any acrobatics. But he has ideas. You know how to make things look good. We'll all just throw in our own kind of flavours and stir it all together and see what comes out. I know it will be something, and I want you in it. Okay? Please, Caramella? C'mon. We can all hang out together.'

She nodded. Still she didn't look at me. I knew she was embarrassed. So I didn't press it. I got another pip and I blew it all the way to the road. I let out a triumphant yell.

'Right on, Mr B.'

Caramella giggled. Right on Mr B., was what my mum said when she got something right. She got it off an ad on tellie where Sammy Davis Junior was trying to sell record players.

Before Caramella went inside, I pointed out the silverbeet that had little drops of glistening Stinky wee on it, and said she better tell her mum to hose it down before they ate it. I would have felt terrible if the Zitos all got sick because of the silverbeet.

# Chapter 26

Before Oscar and Caramella joined us, Kite and I did a week of rehearsals with Kite's dad, who I started to call Ruben. (He told me to.) In the first rehearsal with Ruben, we talked for ages about ideas and moves and how we could find some way of incorporating Oscar and Caramella. Ruben came back to the next one with a plan with all the rehearsals blocked in. Firstly we just had to workshop, he said, just playing around as if it was a game, which meant no getting fussed about what would work and what wouldn't. When we did that, he started to kind of shape the play, make us repeat things or ask us to try it smaller or faster or in slow motion or as if we were dogs, or drunk, or shy, or as if we had strings from our fingers. It was great, because he was much better at spotting than Kite was, and I learned things even quicker with him. After a week, I could do a walkover without any help at all. See, it's all about direction of momentum, pushing forward through your hips and lifting your chest.

Kite and I didn't flop around and talk so much, like we did when we were on our own. We had to concentrate all the time. After a rehearsal, I felt as if I was made of air. And then I'd go home and keep thinking about it, you know, getting big ideas on my bed.

Ruben wasn't like Mrs Mayberry. He wasn't like a normal teacher who just told you things and then gave you tests. He asked us things instead of telling. He was always asking, 'How does that feel? What do you imagine when you do that?'

Kite says, 'I feel curious, very curious.'
I say, 'Like some kind of big prehistoric animal stomping through the long grass.'

'I feel like a plank stuck in mid air.'

Ruben says, 'Can you imagine you are long and light reaching upwards to touch a cloud?'

'Yes.'

'Now, can you fold down over Kite's shoulder?'

'Kite, how do you feel?'

'Like I'm carrying a big sack of potatoes.'

'Push up into the weight. Hold your centre. Try walking as if it's light. Cedar, can you roll round his shoulders and slide down forward, keep contact through your belly, put your hands on his knees? Kite, stand still and drop down through the hips. Hold Cedar's shoulders. I'm wondering, Cedar, if Kite leans back and you lean forward and press your feet towards the ceiling, could you hit a handstand?'

'Great! Can you look at each other as if you're surprised? Surprised to see each other?' (We laugh and lose balance at this point. I flop down over Kite's shoulders again and he shakes me off, down his back.)

'I like that!' says Ruben. 'Shake her off like that, wriggle even more, as if you wanted to get rid of her. Shall we try that whole sequence again? This time, Kite pick Cedar up into the high lift, just as if you were picking something off the ground and putting it up to the light to examine it. Then Cedar, open out as if you were asleep and stretching in the morning. Then, when you see you're in the sky, look alarmed and fold back down to the shoulder.'

Kite looked at me with a new look that I'd never seen

before. He said, 'That was good Cedar. You're getting good. Can you do it again?'

Could I do it again? I was whirling and reeling as if I'd just been hit by a major compliment. That was the first time Kite ever seemed impressed at all. Could I do it again? I could do it a million times more.

*     *     *

Every day, Ruben started by asking us if we had any new ideas or thoughts. It made me feel that my ideas were important. It made me want to keep thinking up things. I told him about how Caramella was artistic, and how I thought she could make designs, and how Oscar had an original mind and had written a book called *Commonplaces* and that maybe he would like to make up some ideas for the show. Kite had this idea of putting Oscar in the centre, like a narrator. I was feeling all puffed-up because Kite had come round to my way of thinking. But I didn't say it. I just grinned a lot and did three cartwheels without stopping.

'What about *Volatile* as a name for the show?' I said.

# Chapter 27

After that week, we had our first rehearsal with Oscar and
Caramella. Caramella came with me and she lagged and
bowed her head and fidgeted with her thumbs and turned
red and pressed her back to the wall. Kite was lying on his
back, warming up, swinging his legs out in full sweeping
circles. Ruben came and shook her hand. She hardly spoke
and wouldn't unglue herself from the wall. Ruben was
arranging mats. I wanted to help lay out the mats but I
didn't want to abandon Caramella to the loneliness of the
wall. Kite's legs swished on the floor, swish, swish, swish. The
sound was somehow menacing, the way it scratched and
itched at the quiet, while Kite seemed to be ignoring the
situation altogether. I felt agitated as hell. I started jigging.

Then, Oscar burst in. He blasted right through the tight
stretched skin of the room, just as if he'd stomped on a
balloon and exploded it. A confused tangle of legs and arms
and there he was blinking, wide-faced and astonished, like a
Martian who had just landed. Caramella unglued herself

from the wall and smiled, because there was someone more awkward than her and everyone was looking at him. I flopped onto my belly in relief and said, 'It's good you're here, Oscar.' Kite stopped his annoying solo leg swishing and leapt up to greet him. It was as if the room, which had been frowning and anxious and awkward, broke into a loose old laugh as Ruben opened his arms wide and welcomed Oscar and suggested we make a circle and talk.

I looked around the circle and thought if we were a soup we'd be one you'd never ever tasted before, one with such an unimaginable blend of flavours that you wouldn't find it in any recipe book, not even a Hari Krishna one. Oscar was wearing his red cape. Caramella concentrated and fiddled and laid her hands over her plump knees while Ruben's grey-cloud eyes shone and leapt about as he talked and asked questions. Kite lounged there in his comfortable way, shooting me one swift look from under his eyelids. I can't tell you what it said, but I felt it as if it bound us together in a secret, satisfied way, for just an instant.

We warmed up at first by playing kids' games, like keepings-off and giant statues. Gradually Caramella began to brim and giggle and burst forward and untie the careful little scared knot in her heart. When it came to trying balances, she was willing and breathless. Oscar kept saying, 'Oh dear,' and frowning and shaking his head. Sometimes he said inexplicable things like, 'Oh it's a traffic jam, now,' and 'Yes I see the landscape, I am reminded of a seagull.' Though he often stumbled, he had a kind of bumbling courage that spilled out like a fizzy drink, sometimes making a big mess, which he'd just wipe off with one awkward elbowed swipe, blinking and booming and stumbling onwards. He made me think of a kind of thirsty explorer battling through low branches, mud and beasts, bravely heading towards something, anything, just onwards. Sometimes he sat down and said, 'Excuse me while I visualise.'

Afterwards, Caramella and I walked home. She was quiet.

'Well, was it okay? Did you like it?' I prodded.

She nodded a large slow nod. 'I'm not very good though, am I? I can't even do a proper handstand.' Caramella tends to be tentative about things. She always needs you to reassure her.

'Yes you can. You just need to practise it.'

'Do you think?'

I nodded. 'You'll just get better.' She swung her hands out a bit and her face looked like she had stuffed a secret inside her pink cheeks.

'Oscar's funny, isn't he?' she said.

'Yep. Funny and brave.'

'Yeah.'

# Chapter 28

After two weeks of workshopping, Ruben came up with an outline. He sat us all together and drew out a plan on a big bit of butcher's paper. I watched him explain it, because he seemed different from when I first met him in the kitchen. Not shy and floppy any more. He was more like a dad – how you'd expect them to be, anyway – tall and strong and leading the show. That's the kind of dad I would've liked to have.

The plan was good. He said he thought we could have a playground theme. We would act out stuff that happens to kids in the playground, only we'd try to put it into a physical language.

'Excuse me, but what do you mean by physical language?' said Oscar, who was wearing his red cape again.

'I mean, say we take something that happens at school, a situation like the way kids might make up a game to play together and that's how they become friends, through playing the game, or imitating . . . Well, we try to represent that situation in acrobatics by making up a kind of game. Maybe it starts with the kind of handshakes kids do and then the handshake becomes a grip, and from the grip there evolves a balance, out and in, out and in. Repetitive. Or double cartwheels, maybe, or a sense of tug of war, like a game. You know, the idea of balance is interesting because you have to trust someone and make a kind of relationship; you depend on them to support you, and they depend on you too, which is the same thing that happens with friends.'

'Ah,' says Oscar wobbling his head a bit and opening his arms wide. 'Let the body speak.'

'Yes. Although not only that – I think of this circus as a type of very physical theatre, which means we bring in many elements. Perhaps we could have you on the stage, acting as the umpire or narrator or supervisor. From there you can call out the rules, only they won't really be rules, they'll be your own commonplaces, from your book. Kite and Cedar can try to physicalise them.'

'What about me?' says Caramella rocking up on her chubby knees.

'Well, apart from the trio balances, I want you to be the stage designer, the costume designer – no – no – the artistic director. Your role is to work with me to design the visual part of the show – how it looks. That's crucial.'

Caramella blushed and puffed up. I was sitting there thinking how everything felt very important, like a conference, like what men in suits do, not an odd bunch of kids and a sad father. I reckoned Harold Barton and Marnie Aitkin and all the other kids had never ever had discussions as important as we were having. Maybe they had, but probably not. Maybe Barnaby had. Which reminded me—

'What about music?' I said.

'Haven't got that far yet. Do you know any musicians who might want to be involved?'

'Only my brother, but he's away.'

'What will the show be called?' said Kite.

'Well that's up to you. Cedar suggested *Volatile*. I thought of a name you could use for your troupe.'

'What?'

'The Acrobrats.'

We all liked that idea. Oscar roared with laughter and fell over backwards.

Chapter 29

The Acrobrats went into full rehearsal and production action.
We didn't get an ad on tellie, because Ruben said it would
cost a lot of money, but he did organise for the local
newspaper to come over and interview us, because that was
free. (Kite says the newspaper came because Ruben is still
known around town.) A photographer took a photo of me
and Kite doing a candlestick balance, and it was on the front
page. The headline said, 'Acrobrats Act For Bambi'.

### AcroBRATS Act For Bambi

Renowned Circus performer, Ruben Freeman, directs
four local youths who have banded together to perform
their own brand of acrobatic theatre in a fundraising
event to be staged next week at a local venue. Funds
from the event will go to a neighbour's dog (Bambi),
who needs an operation in order to survive. See page 2
for inside story.

Page two told more about us. It told about how Ruben was forced to retire from performance due to serious injury. It gave our whole names and talked about Kite being Ruben's son, then it said how such projects should be commended for 'fostering a strong sense of community', for 'bringing together able and disabled bodies', and for 'encouraging youth in positive innovation and creative forms of self-expression'. I don't know quite what they meant by all that, but it sounded important. It gave the date and place. It made us sound like a real company . . .

The Acrobrats perform 'Volatile' on Saturday 20 September, 7p.m. at 45 Hickford St garage. One show only. Enquiries call 9380 4785. Entry by donation.

When I saw us in the newspaper, I felt half excited, half terrified.

'That picture, it made me feel nervous,' I said to Kite, after a rehearsal when everyone else had gone. Kite shrugged.

'Don't worry about it. It's only the local paper – hardly anyone reads that.' He was acting tough. It's a boy thing.

'It makes it seem like a proper show. It makes it real.'

'Well, it will be a proper show.' He stood up and did a beautiful handspring and a bow. 'Now you,' he said, nodding at me as if I was just about to step up onto a horse, while he held the reins. If only it was that easy.

'You know I can't do handsprings,' I sighed.

'No, *you* know you can't do them, whereas *I* know you can. That's the difference. I'll spot you. Remember what Dad says. Shoot your feet up and press from your shoulders.'

I shook my head and screwed up my nose.

'You can do them, Cedy. I can tell. It's only your mind stopping you.'

He called me Cedy. I smiled. It was the first time he'd ever called me that. And then, since I'd accidentally smiled, I kind of had to give it a go. I stood up and helicoptered my arms.

'Picture yourself doing it,' he said, lining himself up on the mat to help. I closed my eyes and tried to imagine my body, doing the beat in, a lean to a skip, and then a snap as the legs arc over and the hands push out of the floor, head coming last, knees bending into the landing . . .

I didn't look at Kite. I just breathed out and willed my body to take over.

It wasn't quite perfect, but it was way closer than I'd ever been. I got over, and the landing was crummy, but both hands came off at once – usually I leave one on, just in case. And Kite hadn't even touched me. I was amazed.

He just laughed and said, 'What did I tell you? By the end of the week you'll be doing them perfectly. You didn't even need me. See, it will be a real show.'

But I could tell he was nervous, too. I could tell by the way he was suddenly very focused, very attentive, not so much mucking about. With only one week to go, and the story in the newspaper, there was a growing sense of urgency about. It made things happen quickly.

✶   ✷   ✷

The next rehearsal, Caramella turned up with a costume for Oscar. It was made of white paper and it was just a long cone shape that covered him from neck to foot. She had painted the walls of the garage white, and drawn a black line across the centre of it and a net shape underneath, like chicken wire. The rest of us would be wearing black T-shirts, since we each had a black T-shirt already, and black shorts which Caramella found at the Salvos. (So much for the glittering dress and the horse – obviously for the next show.) She said the show would be completely in black and white, because it was cheapest and easiest, yet still theatrical, like a Charlie Chaplin movie. We put Oscar in the cone and stood him in the middle. He looked fantastically odd.

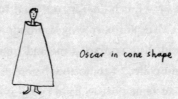

Oscar in cone shape

Ruben loved it. He clapped and said Caramella was a natural born designer, a real artist, and resourceful. He'd never seen such a good design with an almost zero budget.

(He'd paid only twelve dollars for the paint and the shorts.) We all said Caramella was the best. Caramella smiled from one end of her face to the other. With her hands on her hips, she looked almost grown-up. You could tell she'd put a lot of thought into it.

'Yes. Sensational, without being flashy,' said Oscar who always chose his words carefully. 'Stark contrast, bold shapes. I like it. Especially since I'm kind of untouchable here in my paper cone. I've a fragile skin but a strong outline, a strong centre. That's just like me.'

That was true. Oscar's disability made him fragile on the outside, but something strong and true shone through him. Ruben must have been thinking the same thing. He stroked his chin and pursed his lips and had a good idea.

'It would be really good if we could start it in darkness, just Oscar on stage with a light underneath his cone, so that he's shining out like a big lamp.'

Why didn't I think of that? Kite nudged me.

'Cedar and I know where we can get a light,' he said.

'Yes, but how much does it cost?' said Ruben.

'It's free. We're just borrowing it from Cedar's good friend, Harold.' Kite winked at me and I got it. How perfect!

'We could collect it tomorrow, before rehearsal,' I said.

'Great, and remember to hand some of these out at school,' said Ruben, passing us a handful of the fliers that Caramella had made.

# Chapter 30

The next day, before rehearsal, we all went to the hole on our street. Kite brought a steel rod with him for jemmying the lid off. We waited for the street to be quiet and then we set to work. Well, Kite set to work, and we were meant to keep watch. But Caramella went and dragged Oscar over to her house, to get some biscotti. I practised cartwheels on the road. The street is never quiet for long.

'What are you all up to?' came the sing-song voice of Marnie Aitkin as she crept up behind us. The lid had just come off and Kite and I had both bent our heads to peer inside. I looked up at her, then back into the hole. The dark, deep inside seemed way more interesting than a potentially zero conversation with Marnie. Kite lay on his belly and reached down to grab the light. He yanked it out and held it up for us all to see. 'We're just fishing for lights,' he said.

I smothered a giggle and Marnie said, 'Oh sure, very funny.' Then she folded her arms and tapped her foot in an irritating way, as if she was waiting for something else. She

was wearing sneakers with high fat heels. Stupid, I thought
(in my high-and-mighty, superior, know-all way) to
destabilise your sneakers with heels, when sneakers should be
for mucking around in and feeling comfortable. I squinted
pointedly at the shoes and she pressed her well-shaped nose
towards the sky as if she was ignoring us. But she couldn't
help herself.

'Is that yours? You're not meant to open up that hole,' she
said as Kite and I began to examine the light. I could tell she
was annoyed because Kite wasn't paying her any attention at
all, even though her shoes were dramatic. It was brilliant.

'Is now,' I said.

'We saw you in the newspaper, Cedar. If you ask me
that's a pretty stupid reason to do a show – for a dumb dog.'

'No one's asking you,' said Kite, and he lay down again
and squinted and peered and wriggled forward and reached
down into the hole. I could see a yellow patch where the
light shone in on something else.

'What is it?' I said, but before Kite could answer, Marnie,
who was obviously not accustomed to being ignored in
favour of a hole, burst out indignantly, 'Anyway, Kite, if you
hang out with Cedar you better be careful because her
brother's a thief and her dad was a drug addict. Everyone
knows.' Marnie thrust her chin towards me, just as if she was
jabbing a spear at my throat, before she turned on her large
heels and strutted off.

I reared up and shouted at her, 'That's a lie. You're making

it up. You don't know a thing about my dad. Or Barnaby.'
She stopped and turned around.

'Well, that's what Harold Barton says. He says his dad says
so. Barnaby stole Harold's skateboard. For his drugs. Why do
you think Barnaby got sent away then?'

She stuck out her lower lip and put her hands on her
hips, and for a minute I thought I was going to rush up and
slap her. But then I started to cry instead, which was the last
thing I wanted to do, especially in front of Kite. I felt my
mouth wobbling and I couldn't even tell Marnie to go jump.
She looked at me as if she'd just triumphantly snapped shut a
handbag full of money for the bank, and then she strutted
off, wiggling her bum in that fake grown-up way.

A million things rushed through my mind and I couldn't
get hold of one of them. I felt like a bit of paper that had
just been ripped up in pieces and chucked in the wind. I
suddenly wanted to go home and see my mum. I wanted to
disappear. My hands went up and covered my face. Kite put
his hand on my back.

'It isn't true,' I said.

'I know.' Kite bit his lip. I wasn't sure he believed me. He
seemed confused. His eyes were looking past me, as if there
was another bigger thought in view. What did I know really?
Maybe it *was* true. Maybe that was why Mr Barton had
come over all steaming mad. And after that, Barnaby *was* sent
away. And wasn't there all this mystery about my dad and
how he died?

Oscar and Caramella were coming towards us. I didn't want to see anyone. I was all out of focus and ripped up like a bad photo that someone had tossed in the bin. I told Kite I had to go. I couldn't go to rehearsal. I had to go home. He nodded.

Anyway, I didn't even want to be near him if he did believe Marnie Aitkin. I turned and walked quickly away, leaving Kite to explain to the others.

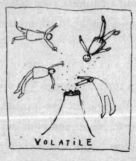

picture of the Flier

# Chapter 31

Strangely enough, when I got home there was a card from Barnaby. He has such timing.

Dear Mum and Cedar, in case you were wondering, I am eating a good breakfast regularly. Yesterday I was on a long bus ride. There was a woman in the seat in front of me. She was old with lavender hair. She was wearing granny nylon slacks, and eating jubes and trying to talk with the bus driver who was just your regular, buoyant, beefy, bus-wielding bloke. She told him a story about her cousin's niece who had just got married. The niece and her new husband went and bought themselves a Chico roll for dinner. When they got home the husband complained that the Chico roll wasn't hot enough. He said he was going to take it back to the shop. The shop was just around the block. So he went. And then he never came back. He died on the way, in an accident. Car accident. That's damn bad luck said the bus driver. Yes, said she, such a shame.

All because of a Chico roll, thought I.
As well as eating a nourishing breakfast I am
avoiding Chico rolls, greater weever fish, poetry
readings, sleeping on couches, working underground,
poisonous mushrooms, tight corners and most
fundamentalists of any kind, especially real estate
agents. I welcome the unknown night within me.
(And the black swan almost next door to me.)
Cedy blue, the mystery is deep around us.


Yep, I thought, getting deeper and deeper. And what
about the black swan? Was she on the bus with him? He
never tells you what you want to know.

I went and got that photo of my dad. He didn't have red
eyes or pin-shaped pupils. He didn't look like a drug addict,
but he didn't look like Mr Barton either. Mr Barton wears a
suit and has a big nose with purple veins running about like
a highway in Los Angeles. My dad just wore a faded old
shirt and a funny hat and his nose is like mine, actually; small
and kind of chubby. His eyes look clear and bright and
good. I can't explain what I mean by good. They were just
crinkled up in a good way. Friendly and true. I got Stinky
and we lay together on the couch, waiting for my mum to
come home. I thought about pulling out of the Acrobrats.
I imagined them all sitting around and Kite telling them
how I came from a bad family of drug addicts and thieves.
Caramella wouldn't believe it. She knew Barnaby. I knew
Barnaby. He wasn't a thief. I knew that.

Well, stuff the circus, I didn't want to be in it, anyway. If they thought I was a bad person then let them do it without me. I had better things to do. I might just run away myself. I'd go and find Barnaby. I'd bring him back and he'd tell me, he'd tell me just what went on and then I'd tell them. I'd tell Marnie and Harold and everyone. I'd write a goddamn essay about it and I'd nail it up to the lampposts. I'd hang upside-down from the plane trees and write it on my tummy in thick black texta and draw attention to myself by singing the Lord's Prayer in Egyptian. I'd skateboard up and down the street, yelling out like an orphan newspaper boy. I know all about it. I know all about it.

Yeah, we'd find Barnaby. Me and Stinky, we'd go together. To Perth. On the train. That night. Before anyone could stop me.

'How about it, little hairy beast?' I said to Stinky, who was gnawing at his rump and feeling quite smug about being on the couch.

I leapt up, suddenly inspired by my solution. For just an instant I was excited. I jigged and paced and tried to get practical, but it's always hard to be sensible when you're feeling emotional and blurry. Stinky stared at me with a worried look. All I could know for sure was that if I didn't get going soon, Mum would be home and then there'd be no hope of me going anywhere.

I packed a bag; five pairs of favourite undies, three pairs of socks without holes, trackies, corduroy skirt, singlets,

T-shirts and cardigan, sloppy joe, sunnies, beanie, mossie bite
balm, toothbrush, Oil of Ulan for prevention of wrinkles,
my new Palace Music CD to impress Barnaby, photo of my
dad (for the drama of it), photo of my mum (in case I never
came back), *God Bless Love* (favourite book from when I was
a kid), *Lucetius, On the Nature of the Universe* (a book of
Barnaby's that he hadn't read yet and that I planned to read
about half of on the train and to memorise certain quotes
that I would let drop, at seasonable moments, when I got to
Perth – the idea being that Barnaby would see how I had
become alarmingly wise and mature, and as a result he
would be more easily persuaded to return with me. What a
plan! Boy! What a sophisticated plan!).

Also in the suitcase (which the bag had now become), I
stuffed a frosted glass pig full of coins, electric clock radio, jar
of holy water from the Holy Mother, loaf of bread and a jar
of honey, bread board, bones for Stinky, a red plastic whistle,
diary, torch, and scissors – because you never know when
you might need scissors.

It was way too heavy.

I took out the bread board.

And the piggy bank.

And the scissors.

Fed Stinky some of the bones.

Wrote a short theatrical note to Mum. 'Mum, I've gone.'
Then we left the house.

# Chapter 32

It was that time when the day begins to turn into night.
When the sky gets deep and glowing with the last bit
of light. When the night plonks little sooty clouds in the sky.
When there are smudges of yellow light coming out from
windows, peeking under curtains and doors. When there are
cars murmuring home and people turning in their gates
with keys jingling in pockets and bags. When there are kids
getting off the street and people are cooking spaghetti or
chops, or leaving offices, and televisions are purring away in
living rooms telling the news in a tidy way.

That's how it was when I left the house. It was going-
home time.

I could only walk about twenty-three steps before I had
to stop and put down my suitcase, which was still too heavy.
I could smell mashed potato and fried fish coming out of
the boys' house. I saw Mr Barton drive his car up the
driveway. The headlights shone on the house for a moment
and I could see the box hedges in a line next to the brick

walls, and then the lights went off and I couldn't see anything. The trees in the street had papery leaves which trembled on the branches.

I was getting a funny feeling. I wouldn't say scared, no I wouldn't say that, but something pretty close. The word 'homesick' sat in my throat like a big gobsucker. Could I be homesick already, only fifty paces down the street? I was ashamed of myself. What a sook, what a baby! I picked up my suitcase and dragged it onwards, thinking soldier, thinking Robert de Castella, thinking Hercules. Stinky trotted along like a little breeze. Obviously he had no idea that we were actually leaving home. Let me tell you, it's harder running away when you really mean it.

I wondered how Barnaby had felt when he left. I tried to picture it. For one thing, he would have been singing himself a song, a comforting, encouraging friendly travelling song. I tried to think of one, but all I could think of was *Eleanor Rigby*.

It had a deserted feeling about it.

I put my suitcase down again, since my shoulder was getting sore. I sat on the case and concentrated on the chorus,

> *all the lonely people*
> *where dooo they all come from?*

because I can never hit the dooo note right, so I need to concentrate.

Out of the corner of my eye, even in the midst of my

singing, I recognised a tall dark figure approaching. It was
the walk – unmistakable. One leg straight and dragging, the
long body leaning away from the dragging leg, a slight
hiccup in the opposite shoulder. Most of all, a sense that at
any moment the long tilting shape could topple over –
though it didn't. It was Oscar.

> *all the lonely people*
> *where dooo they all belong?*

Oscar? What was he doing lurching down my street,
about to stumble across me and my suitcase and my faltering
attempt at escape? He waved; his whole arm thrashed wildly
in the night air. I stopped singing and waved limply back.
Definitely sprung. I put my head in my hands and tried to
find an explanation. *I'm on my way to stay with a crotchety aunt
who has sugar diabetes and needs me to take bread and honey?* Oh
hell, I thought, and what did Oscar think of me anyway, now
that Kite had told them all about my disreputable drug-
influenced immoral family?

'Cedar! You look dishevelled,' said Oscar. He towered
above me, with his face like a moon. He clutched a brown
envelope tied with string.

'Dishevelled? Do I?' I felt pathetic. Flattened-out. Stinky
sniffed Oscar's hand.

'Yes. Kite told us you weren't feeling well.' He looked
concerned.

'Did he? Did he say why?'

'No. But he was worried about you.'

'Oh. I'm all right now.' I smiled up at him and he smiled back. Then it was quiet, except for the distant rumble of traffic and the scratch of leaves scurrying into gutters. Oscar never seemed to be bothered about quiet breaks in conversation. He just continued leaning and wobbling there in the dark air above me, as if that's normal. And I guess it is. You shouldn't always have to say something. Generally I do, though.

'So, Oscar, what brings you here?'

'Bringing you this.' He thrust the envelope towards me. 'I was just going to put it in your letterbox. To make you feel better. It's just a drawing I did for you.'

'For me?'

'Yeah. Because you weren't well. So I went home and did it.' He folded his hands and grinned.

'That's nice of you.' I felt suddenly like I was about to cry again. But I didn't let myself. I held my breath instead. 'Shall I open it now?'

'Yes. If you like.'

I didn't really want to open it then and there, in case it made me feel funny again, but I did anyway, because it seemed that I should. This is what the drawing looked like. I still have it today, stuck up on my wall, because it means a lot to me. Whenever I feel hopeless I look at that drawing.

'That's you in the middle,' said Oscar, placing his finger on the spot.

a five tree balance

'Because you're like the centre part of things, you're in the middle of the web. That's why I drew it like that. That's how it feels. And if you weren't here we'd all fall down.'

'No, if anyone wasn't here, we'd all fall down.'

'Yeah. That's true too. It's lucky we're all here, isn't it?'

'Yeah, it is.'

'Cedar, I think you . . . ' he stopped and blinked. 'I mean, you planted seeds. Did you ever think what a thing could grow? You have a green thumb for people. That's why there are trees in the drawing.'

I smiled and I buried my heart in that drawing, and if it hadn't been so dark you might have noticed me glowing, just a little.

'Well, I'll see you tomorrow, Cedar,' said Oscar, still grinning and glancing about.

'Yeah, see ya.' I couldn't begin to explain to him all the feelings that were having a raging battle inside me. The noise of them caught me like a light catches an animal in the night, making it dumb and still. My eyes opened out wide trying to see what was battling what. I wanted to say something. I wanted to tell him that he was special and the drawing was especially special, but I couldn't say it. I didn't say anything.

He beamed anyway, and stumbled off down the street, and I watched him go. He hadn't even asked me what the hell I was doing sitting on a suitcase in the dark street singing *Eleanor Rigby* to a small hairy dog. Oscar never seemed to notice what was ordinary and what wasn't ordinary.

Yet he had another sense, an extra-ordinary sense. Or did he? Did he just happen to wander down my street and bump into me, and just happen to make me feel like I should stay and see this circus through? He didn't even know. He didn't even know what that drawing meant to me. But he'd done the drawing. He didn't even know I was running away. But he'd delivered it at exactly the right moment.

Sometimes life hits you at such a startling lightning kind of angle, that you get pushed off your normal viewing spot. You stop knowing how things are. Instead of what you know, there are the patterns that stars make; the sound of the night breathing; the small aching spot where your feet touch the earth . . . And you've never felt closer to it. You think that if there is an It, you and It are nearly touching. You feel religious and devoted and tiny. Just for a moment you feel as if the whispering coming from the leaves and beetles and sky and footsteps and sighs is going directly towards *your* ear. So you listen.

There, sitting on a suitcase, next to a stinky dog, in a suburban street in Brunswick, I had one of those moments. What I heard was Life telling me to go back and, as they say in the movies, face the music. Go home, it said. Go home.

To tell you the truth, I was kind of relieved, since I was hungry anyway. I sat there for just a respectful moment more, and then I dragged that suitcase back home, trying to think of a likely story to tell Mum.

# Chapter 33

Mum was so relieved to see me, she forget to get angry. I didn't even need to tell her why I went; she thought it was her fault. She thought she wasn't a good-enough mother. She sat me down and tried to explain how she was doing two jobs at once; she was working hard so that we could one day buy our own house, and she was trying to be a mother as well. And it was hard doing two things at once, and being a mother and a father (which made three jobs, really), and she wanted to be there when I got home from school and she wanted to cook me a good dinner every night, and she wanted to spend more time with me, and with Barnaby too . . . And then she was crying, and the funny thing was, it was me comforting her and saying it was okay, I understood. I promised I wouldn't run away, and I promised Barnaby would come home soon. Who was I to promise that? But you do say extravagant things when you want to comfort someone. I didn't ask Mum about Dad or Barnaby, because she was already so sad and jumbled-up.

So we went out to Cleopatra's and ate falafel, and she asked me lots of questions about the circus and I could tell she was trying hard to be a good mother. She didn't need to, but I let her anyway. I think it made her feel better. And I felt better, too. I love falafel. But not with raw onions.

✴ ✴ ✴

The next day was Saturday and I did my best to sleep in. I kept my eyes shut and tried not to think any thoughts. But the harder I tried the more they kept coming at me. I was getting all tangled up in thoughts.

There was a banging at the door. I got up. It couldn't be Mum. I knew she was still in bed. And Ricci never knocks – she just yells out your name from outside until you come. Caramella always comes in through the kitchen door. In fact hardly anyone knocks on our door, just the Mormons with their Jesus stories or Mr Barton with his thumping fist.

It was Kite.

'What are you doing here?' I said. Stinky wagged his tail. If I'd had a tail I wouldn't have wagged it, but dogs don't get moody or rude. At least, Kite hadn't gone and squealed to everyone about those ugly rumours.

'Look, I didn't know what to say, before. See, I was confused about it, didn't know what it meant. But I worked it out and I have to tell you.'

'Tell me what?'

'Look, was it a yellow skateboard with a drawing of a skull on it — Harold's one that was stolen?'

'Yeah.'

'Well, in the hole, the other thing, it was that skateboard. I figured it might have been when that horrible girl was saying your brother stole it.' (I can't help noticing here that Kite doesn't even remember Marnie Aitkin's name.) 'But then I worked out it couldn't have been Barnaby who put it there because, firstly, why would he steal it if he just wanted to put it in a hole? And, secondly, I remembered that we saw Harold putting the light in the hole, so Harold must have seen the skateboard in there. He *knew* it was there and he didn't say, which makes me think he must have put it in there in the first place. Harold must have hidden it and then told his dad that Barnaby took it. Did he have it in for your brother?'

Boy, he'd really thought it out. Oh, it all made sense, suddenly. The yellow thing in the hole. Harold ratting on Barnaby.

'Yes!' I almost shouted. And then you know what I did? I was so relieved, I threw my arms around Kite's neck — not for long, just for an instant — and then I laughed, half to cover the fact of having almost bumped foreheads in that awkward sudden hug, half because I always laugh when some tension is let out, like a balloon going crazy when air whooshes out of it. Don't worry — I instantly composed myself and moved quickly along by explaining how I knew Harold Barton was jealous as hell of Barnaby, because

Barnaby's a natural. Barnaby's good at footy – even Harold's
dad said so. And he's even better at skateboarding than
Harold, though Barnaby never even had his own board –
he just had a go on other people's. But by far the most
aggravating thing about Barnaby is that he doesn't even care
about all that; he doesn't care about being good at footy;
he doesn't brag, he doesn't even want to be in the Zebras,
even though the Zebras want him. What he really likes is,
music, and thinking up ideas, and some girls, but not many
of them . . . So, anyway, Mr Barton must have come huffing
over here and accused Barnaby of stealing his son's
skateboard, so Mum sent Barnaby away to boarding school.

'Goddamn!' said Kite.

'Yeah,' I said, and we both shook our heads and thought
bad thoughts about Harold, together. After a few nice
moments of sharing our distaste for Harold Barton, Kite said
he better go, and reminded me that we only had four
rehearsals left before the show.

'I'll be there. Sorry about missing it yesterday,' I said.

'No worries.' He stretched his arms up and hung for a
minute from the doorway. I could see his belly button. And
the muscles in his belly. My hand wanted to tickle him, but I
didn't let it. Then he went.

☆    ☆    ☆

That night, Mum got home later than usual, but she had
pizza. She brings home pizza when she feels bad for coming

home so late. She knows pizza will always turn me from a grump into an angel.

'Did you get half without anchovies?' I said, because she loves anchovies and I hate them. My mum is mostly vegetarian, except when it comes to anchovies on pizza and calamari rings fried in batter. Those things she can't resist.

'Of course,' she said triumphantly. And she threw off the lid and slid the pizza under my nose for inspection.

'You're late,' I said with just exactly the right amount of grumpiness, enough to show that she hadn't got away with it completely but not so much that I might appear unbribable by the very glorious pizza bribe.

'Sorry,' she grimaced. 'It was work. But, Cedy, I'm negotiating. I'm trying to get my hours changed, so if I work a long Saturday I can get off earlier some week nights and come home earlier.'

It wasn't as if I'd been angling for Mum to do that, but since I'd tried running away, she'd decided it would be a good thing. So I decided it would be, too, especially if it meant that she wouldn't be so tired when she got home, so then I could ask her questions without giving her a headache.

We sat down at the table and we didn't even bother with plates. I love that. I ate two whole pieces pretty quickly without hardly speaking, then halfway through the next slice I started the conversation.

'Mum?'

'Yes.'

'Was Dad a drug addict?'

She put down her slice of pizza. Her mouth dropped open.

'No, of course he wasn't. Why do you ask?'

'Mr Barton said he was. He told Harold, and Harold told the other kids.'

'Mr Barton was wrong to say that. Listen, sweetheart, Mr Barton and your dad were very different kinds of people. Your dad was a leftie and Mr Barton—'

'What's a leftie?'

She took a deep breath. 'A leftie is someone who believes that – well they believe in sharing. They're not always good at sharing in their personal life' – she gave a little odd smile – 'but in politics they believe that the government should make sure there is enough for everyone, so that all people can afford basic things like housing and education and healthcare. Often, you see, a very few people end up with much much more than they need, while many many people don't have nearly enough.'

'What do righties believe then? Don't they think sharing is good?'

She laughed. 'They're not called righties, they're called conservatives or capitalists. Or today they're part of a way of thinking that is called economic rationalism. Look, I'm not very political myself so I can't explain this very well, but basically, the Mr Bartons in this world believe that things work best if people are encouraged to make as much money as they can in whatever way they want. They think this money will create jobs and trickle down to the people who don't have enough. The problem is that the money may be made in ways that are harmful to both the environment and the spirit of society. And often it doesn't trickle down at all.'

'What do you mean – the spirit of society?'

'I guess I'm talking about happiness, real happiness, not the kind that comes from money and new cars or swimming pools. Real happiness comes from loving your family and friends, from caring for other people, or from communicating something to another person, or just from singing a song you like . . . It sounds a bit sappy, but you know what I mean?'

'Yes. Like making a circus show?'

'Yes, like that.'

'Doesn't Mr Barton care for other people?'

'Of course he does. It's just that many big businesses are doing very uncaring things because it makes them a lot of money. Not all business is bad though. There are people who earn a good living through good businesses. Like that bakery in Brunswick where they make that organic sourdough bread we like. And Mr Barton isn't bad. He just might feel threatened by anyone who wants to make changes. Now, your father was involved with the Green Movement. Anyone who fights to save trees and forests is often seen as a hippy or a drop-out – someone who smokes pot and sings protest

songs. That's why Mr Barton says your dad was a drug addict
– only because he felt threatened by what your father was
doing.'

'Oh.'

'Does that make sense to you, Cedar?' She leaned her
head towards me, looking worried.

'Yep. I think so.' I started on the rest of the pizza. She
smiled. I wasn't sure I really understood it all. It seemed very
complicated. I don't like economics or politics. It just seems
to cause a lot of arguments. But as far as I could see, my dad
was on the good side, the sharing side. And I was satisfied. I
planned to ask more some day, but that was enough for one
night.

I had other things to think about for the next four days.

Chapter 34

Ironically, the self-stolen skateboard of Harold Barton, which we innocently fished out of the hole, became a crucial prop in our show. We attached a rope to either end and got Oscar standing on top of it. Caramella lengthened the cone costume, so it came right down over the board and you couldn't see that he was standing on anything. But we could move him along by pulling the rope. At one stage, Kite and I had a tug of war over Oscar. It looked tricky and great.

I told Kite about my dad being a leftie and a greenie and not at all a drug addict. He said he thought Ruben was a leftie, too, and we decided that if we ever had to be anything, other than an acrobat, we might be lefties, too. But I hoped it wouldn't come to that.

Ricci read the newspaper article. She came over and wrapped her arms around me saying, 'I love you, you an angel.' She hugged me for ages, and I was stuck with my face squashed up against her drooping breasts.

The night before the show, it started to rain like mad.

It howled down all over the roof and roads and trees.
The world seemed to be trembling under the blanket of
rain. I lay in bed thinking and thinking and ordering myself
to go to sleep, and worrying because of the animals that
might be stuck outside, and because the rain might break
through the blotchy yellow ceiling above me and because
I'd be tired tomorrow so I'd surely stuff-up and fall or
forget what to do. I ordered myself to go to sleep, and I
tried thinking of something else, like my dad the leftie,
and how I must remember to hold my tummy inwards
for balance.

A loud banging woke me right up. My heart was
thumping in my chest. I could feel it. Did I imagine that
noise? The rain clattered and wooshed on the roof. Maybe
I was asleep after all and it was just my dream. But then I
heard it again! Bang Bang Bang! An urgent, purposeful
sound. I sat very still, too frightened to move. Stinky growled
from his basket. I called his name quietly and he jumped up
onto the bed. We sat there and listened. The room was dark,
full of dim colourless shapes; a cupboard, clothes huddled
over a chair, Stinky's basket, bookshelf, door. Was the door
moving? Rain clattered on the window but I glued my eyes
to the door. I could feel my skin going prickly. The door
handle turned. Suddenly all I could hear was myself
breathing. I ducked down under the covers and squeezed my
eyes shut. I was probably about to be murdered and I didn't
want to see it.

I could hear the someone creeping towards my bed.
A hand landed on my body. I went stiff. Was it a big hairy
hand? Take anything, I thought, take my piggy bank, take my
instamatic camera, take my . . .

'Cedar, are you awake?' It was Mum.

'You scared me.'

'Sorry, I didn't mean to, but was that you whacking the
wall again? I heard a banging.'

'No, it wasn't me. I heard it, too.' Even she looked scared
then. She sat on my bed and thought a while. I'd never seen
my mother look frightened before. I could tell she was
trying not to let me know because she kept holding my arm
and squeezing out a smile, but mostly she concentrated on
listening. Her mouth was half open, as if it was about to
receive a sharp gulp of air. I wished we had a dad here. We
were both listening hard to see if it would come again. I
prayed that *it* whatever *it* was, had gone. Then Mum said she
thought she'd better go and look.

'You're not leaving me here alone. I'm coming with you.'

'Well put something warm on.'

I turned the light on and grabbed a jumper and some
socks. 'Shouldn't we just call the police? Get them to go and
look?'

'Well, maybe. In any case we have to get to the phone.'

Just then a big clod of earth smashed against my window.
There was a whistle. A little tune. Stinky wagged his tail and
trotted over to the window. Mum and I stared at each other.

We were both suddenly thinking and knowing the same thing. We raced over to the window and yanked it up, leaning out into the dark backyard.

'Barnaby? Is that you?' yelled Mum. We could just make out a person standing in the middle of the long grass of our backyard.

'Yeah, Mum. I'm back. Sorry to arrive at such a damn dark hour. Couldn't help it.' He opened his arms wide. 'Hi, Cedy Blue. Look at this! I'm back in time for the show.'

I practically squealed. I ran to the back door and flung it open. Barnaby stood there grinning. His guitar was leaning against him and he hadn't shaved. He looked rough and messed up and wet as a drowned dog but devilishly handsome. My mum always said Barnaby had a Robert Redford jaw, but I never thought about it before. Mum came up and hugged him.

'Oh, I'm so glad you're home,' she said, like a big sap. I could tell by her voice that she was going to cry a bit. 'My god, you're soaked, you'd better get those wet clothes off.'

I wasn't going to cry. I was feeling madly happy.

'How'd you know about the show?' I demanded, determined to switch his attention to me. Barnaby turned and gave me a big squeeze and I gave him a big squeeze back. We never used to hug. We usually just had tickle fights. But Barnaby seemed old enough to be like a grown-up, not just a brother.

'Yuk, you're wet and cold.'

Barnaby shook and stamped like Stinky does after you
bath him.

'Stinky boy!' said Barnaby, and picked up Stinky who was
wagging like mad and letting off indignant little yelps.

'Well, how'd you know?' I insisted.

'Yes,' said Mum, 'tell us.'

Barnaby flopped onto a kitchen chair with Stinky on his
lap.

'Well, bit of a long story. I was actually on my way to
Darwin. I'd caught a bus to Adelaide and from there I'd
hitched a ride with a truck driver who'd come from
Melbourne. His name was Edgar T. Mozart (no relation), and
he was taking a load of fridges up through the Centre.
Anyway, we get talking, and turns out he lives in Brunswick,
just up on Macfarland Street, and he'd just come from home
and then – whaddya know? – it so happens he's got the local
paper on the dash. He points it out to me and for a while I
don't even think of looking at it, but later on, after the talk
has died down, I pick it up just for something to read, and
lo and behold, who should I see on the front cover but our
own Cedy Blue, looking quite spectacular, I must say. So I
get the surprise of my life. I read the article and I notice that
the show is on the next night. I explain things to Edgar T.
Mozart who is a completely great bloke. When I tell him I
have to jump out and find a ride back to Adelaide, the guy
just turns around and drives me back. We'd gone about an
hour out. Not only that, he gives me a ten bucks to

contribute to your cause. Said he wished he could come to
the show, but he's gonna ring the wife and kids and tell
them to come. What a guy, huh? So anyway, from Adelaide
I hitched back here. That's why I arrived so late. Trams have
stopped. I got dropped in Flemington. Had to walk. I'm
stuffed.' He let out a big yawn.

'Thanks, Barn, thanks for coming all the way back.' I
looked down and said it quietly because I felt shy and gooey
and I wasn't sure how it would come out. I didn't think
anything would really come out the way it should, like the
huge way I felt about Barnaby coming back for me.

'Oh, you're a worry to me!' said Mum, and gave him
another hug. Then she said he had to get into a hot bath,
quick as possible, and I had to get to sleep quick as possible,
and we could finish our conversation in the morning.
I protested, but she pointed out that it was two o'clock in
the morning and the big night tomorrow and so the rest
could wait.

'What rest?' I whispered to Barnaby as we went off to
bed. 'Does she mean the black swan?'

He grinned and ruffled my hair but I didn't care since
I was only going to bed anyway. 'Not just the black swan,
Cedy Blue, there's also the rest.'

There's always more, I thought, and I sighed in my
superior know-all way.

# Chapter 35

I must have slept deeply, because when I woke up Mum and
Barnaby were already awake. The rain had calmed down
and I could hear them talking in the kitchen. I could smell
cigarettes and coffee. By the deep rumbly continuous sound
of the voices I knew they'd been going at it for yonks and
I'd been missing out. I rubbed my eyes to make it look
like I'd been awake too, and then I got out of bed and went
to the kitchen. I stopped at the door and listened. There was
a hushed insistent sound to the voices.

'You have to tell her, Mum,' Barnaby was saying. 'She
should know the truth. She's old enough to know.'

'Yes, you're probably right. She's been asking questions.
I've been putting it off, I know. But not today? Not with the
show. She's nervous enough about that. It's enough for her to
think about. And you being here, too.'

'Okay, not today. Look, do you want me to tell her?'

'No, no, it's bad enough that you had to find out
elsewhere. I'll tell her myself.'

'She'll be okay, Mum. She's not a kid any more.'

'Yes.'

There was a quiet pause. I heard a chair groan as someone got up.

'You want another coffee?' I could tell by the light tone in Mum's voice that she had no intention of resuming talk on that same deadly serious topic. But then just when I thought all seriousness was over, out came a little speech.

'Barn, honey, I feel like I've made some mistakes with you and Cedy. I want to explain. See, when your father died, I panicked about security. So I've been working long hours because I want to get us our own house one day. It was what I thought would be the best thing I could give to you kids. Your own house. That was what we wanted, your father and I. But lately, I've been seeing how maybe it wasn't what you needed as much as just time, my time.'

There was a moment of quiet. Then Barnaby said, 'Yeah, maybe.' I think he was embarrassed. And then there was quiet again. There was a sigh and Mum said mmmm and started scratching around for something, probably a lighter. Then again it went quiet. All those quiet pauses were making me uncomfortable and I wasn't even there.

'Well do you think I should wake Cedy? She's doing a walk-through at twelve-thirty,' said Mum.

'I'll wake her,' said Barnaby and I heard him stand up and give the table leg a good kick back into place. I stepped into the kitchen and rubbed my eyes in a fake sleepy way, this time to make it look like I *was* just waking up.

'Well, look who's awake,' said Mum. 'Just in time for some brekkie before your rehearsal. Do you want toast?'

'Yes please. When did you two get up?' I acted a bit grumpy and snoozy. I flopped over to the bread bin and dropped two slices in the toaster. Mum put a plate on the table, to make sure I used one.

'A while ago. Feeling like a champion, Cedy?' said Barnaby.

'No.'

'Bummer.'

'What have you two been talking about? Did I miss much?' I said, trying not to sound suspicious.

'Oh, only the complete, unabridged, undiminished, unrevised, uncut version of my spontaneous, self-initiated, extended vacation.' Barnaby rocked back on the chair with his arms behind his head and chuckled. His arms were bigger than they used to be.

'You forgot unrepeatable,' I said, buttering my toast vigorously.

'Barn, you'll break that chair,' said Mum.

'So I missed the black swan chapter then?' I said, pulling the crusts off my toast.

'Ah, now that, that's very repeatable,' said Barnaby, and I could almost see his mind sail far away out of the kitchen and back in time. It made his eyes go soft and his smile go

slow and dreamy, and I had to roll my eyes and chuck the
Wettex at him, which made him laugh.

'And why didn't you tell us where you were?' I
demanded.

'Why don't you kids eat your crusts?' said Mum, frowning
for a moment as she spread the Saturday papers over the
table, taking up all the room.

'Ah, Mum, you know, crusts are for Rita and Door.
They love 'em more,' said Barnaby, chucking the crusts in
the compost bin. 'Hey, Cedar, you should have an egg,
for protein, so you feel strong tonight.'

'Don't wanna egg. I gotta go now, anyway.'

'Shall I walk you there?'

'Okay.'

*   *   *

We walked up the street, and Barnaby asked about the
Lebbos and Ricci and Caramella and even the Bartons.

'And how's Harold Barton; what new toy has Harold
got?'

'He's got the latest Play Station,' I said, and Barnaby
chuckled. He gestured to the boys' nice satisfied house and
said, 'And do the fancy-pants still think we're ferals?'

'Yep,' I said proudly, because even though Mum didn't
like it, I couldn't care less if they thought we were wild like
foxes. Anyway, Robert still helped me with my broken rib,
so he wasn't bad, just a snob.

We walked along the Merri Creek. It smelt muddy and
old and the water was rushing milky brown because of the
rain. There were brown ducks getting borne along, whether
they wanted to or not, and we could see a Twistie packet
twisting and turning as it was swept downstream. I said, if
I was a Twistie packet, that's how I'd like to end my days —
dancing gloriously and quietly in a merry creek. Barnaby
said that if he was a Twistie packet, he'd be tucked away
in the pocket of Walt Whitman or Bob Dylan, and he'd
be travelling around America, looking out and listening.
'But Walt Whitman's dead,' I said, and he said, 'So is a
Twistie packet.' Stinky barked at the ducks, but the ducks
just kept on doing their duck business, which was mainly
just body surfing the rush, hoping a fish might float near
their mouths.

'Where will they end up?' I said.

'In another duck country,' said Barnaby.

We saw the rabbit man in the distance, but we didn't talk
to him. We were too busy talking to each other. We went
and sat under the cooing bridge and I told Barnaby about
my Pat and Gary theory, and then we worked out that
Barnaby had been away for sixteen months, which is more
than a year. Mostly he'd been in Western Australia, where he
had lots of different odd jobs — only for getting by, not for
anything else, though once he got a job working for a
documentary film maker who was making a film about
tortoises, and he liked that. We walked on.

'Why did you go to Western Australia, anyway?' I asked.

He paused and frowned and looked at the ground, though there was nothing on the ground except lines which you should tread on if you want good things to happen to you.

'Well, I guess because there were things I wanted to find out.'

'What kind of things?'

'About our dad. His brother lives there.'

'I didn't know he even had a brother.'

'No, there's a bit you don't know.'

Aha, I thought, here we go. The serious topic at breakfast. Did I want to know? Barnaby seemed pained. I felt a bit anxious and fuzzy. I had to know.

'What things?' I put my hand on my tummy.

'Look, Mum really wanted to explain this all to you later, after the show, but since it's come up now, I can tell you now if you want me to.'

I stopped walking and stood still in a serious kind of stance. I put on my low, almost adult voice.

'Barnaby, I know stuff. I know about the skateboard. I know you didn't steal it. Harold hid it in the hole. And I know Dad was a leftie.'

'How did you know all that?' Barnaby smiled and I felt a bit better. I told him how I knew, and he laughed a lot. Then we sat on the grass and he told me what he found out from our new uncle in Western Australia.

Barnaby said there were things Mum never told us, because of the problems between her and Dad. For one thing, Dad wasn't a musician, like I thought he was, not seriously anyway; he just fooled around singing. What he was really passionate about was saving trees and forests, but that caused a lot of problems between Mum and him because he wasn't at home much. He was always off organising protests and trying to stop logging, working for the Wilderness Society. Mum believed in what he was doing, but she also felt let down by him, because he seemed to care more about the forests than his own family. He sometimes went away for weeks, staying at demonstrations in the Otways. If he was chained to a tree, she couldn't contact him at all. When I was born, he was away, in the mountains or having a meeting with the government or something. Granma had to take Mum to the hospital, and Barnaby had to be looked after by the neighbours because we couldn't afford a babysitter for the thirty-seven hours that I took in coming out. Mum had me all on her own.

So, though he was a good guy in one way — yes, in a very big and right way, as Barnaby put it — he painted himself into a picture of such admirable and epic proportions that he had no paint left to work on the small details. Like the little family that needed him. So it was a noble painting which lacked depth. Barnaby said he just had a job which demanded more than regular jobs, because what he was doing was urgent. But my mum always felt second-best.

So they fought a lot, even though they did love each other, and he did love us, too. When he had time.

And then, when I was only about one or something, I went and crawled off the edge of someone's balcony and landed in a garden. Mum rushed me to hospital, because she thought I might have brain damage. (Praise the heavens that Barnaby didn't get hold of that one when we were kids.) She was distraught (of course), and while I was having tests she rang our father, who was in the Otways, and said he had to come home *now* because she needed him. It was a crisis. She wasn't coping on her own. Well, he came straightaway, but he was tired from being up all night, and it was a curly drive around the mountain. That was really how he died – not of a heart attack, but from an accident. No one knows what happened exactly, but his car went off the side of the road. And my mum suffered terribly; not just from grief, but also from guilt, because she felt she shouldn't have demanded that he come back. But she was so tired of always having to manage on her own.

We sat there in silence on the grass by the creek. The first clear thought that came to my mind was that I was going to be late. But I couldn't quite move. I felt as if the inside parts of me were being slowly rearranged; as if the structures in my mind, all the framework that I'd been leaning my thoughts and feelings on, were being rearranged. It was a heavy, slow feeling, like what a house must feel when one of its walls has been smashed down and another kind of wall is being built. Amidst all the hammering and smashing I could only make out that one clear pillar of thought – the thought that I'd be late – because everything else was in shambles. My mind felt like a cloud of dust hovering over a mess of broken plaster walls.

So my dad was good and bad. I guess it always depends on who's looking and from what angle. After all, everyone has their own angle to look from, and no one has perfect corners to be looked at, except maybe Jesus Christ or Mother Teresa or Marge Manoli, the Op Shop mother, but I bet even they did one or two questionable things along the way. Anyway, I didn't want to worry about my dad's corners, because he wasn't here. My mum was here and she had to work hard to look after us. No wonder she was often tired and cranky, and boy I loved her for sticking around. I really did. And with that thought, I felt tears balling up in the corner of my eyes.

'Why didn't Mum tell us? Why did she say he had a heart attack?' I wiped my eyes with my finger.

Barnaby was looking out at the creek, pulling at the grass with his hand.

'Because at the time it was simpler. I was five years old and you were only a baby. She thought it was too complicated for me to understand, or too traumatic. Besides, she wanted to move away from it. That was when we moved in with Granma, and Mum started a new life. She wanted to move on. She always planned to tell us when we were old enough, but then it never came up, till now, because I found out.'

'I'm not mad at her. I'm mad at our dad.'

'Yeah, I know, but you gotta remember he was young. He was only twenty-five; that's only six years older than me. And he helped save a lot of old growth forests – that's important – that's something to be proud of. He couldn't have done that if he was always at home. And he was good when he was around. I remember that. He used to sing to us. He was funny.'

'I'm going to be late.'

'I know. You okay?'

'Yep.' Was I? I stood up and the ground felt the same as always. I was glad about that. But I had an angry feeling inside me. It was as if my mind had rolled itself up into a big stone poised and looking for a place to fling itself. But at what? At the mountain curve my dad drove off; at my dad who was coming home because of me; at me for causing a crisis; or at life for not being one straight unbumpy road, but always throwing you a bend you can't get round?

And since I couldn't throw that anger anywhere, it started crumbling a bit and faltering, and my head dropped, and I saw my feet in their grubby sneakers standing there on the path. I rocked up on my toes and back on my heels and back on my toes. I kept rocking like that for a long moment. I was deciding . . . I don't know what I was deciding. I just had a feeling that I could tip one way or another, and it was up to me.

At least I thought, it was clear now. It was as if some murky part of me had just gone clear, like an open window. I could see out through it properly, and I knew how things were, how they looked and felt. I didn't necessarily like the view (well, I never would have chosen that view) but at least it was something that wouldn't go or change or die. And Barnaby was back, and Mum was at home reading the Saturday Extra, like always, and Kite and Ruben and Caramella and Oscar were all waiting for me, and we were still the Acrobrats, no matter what my dad did or didn't do all those years ago.

As they say in the movies, the show must go on!

# Chapter 36

When I got there, we did a couple of walk-throughs and then Ruben gave us each a pair of socks with our names printed on one side and Acrobrats printed on the other. He said it was a tradition to give presents to the cast before a show. Caramella had two packets of biscotti from her mum, for us to share. There was also a big bunch of flowers for us all. Purple irises with a card which said 'Thank you, from Ricci'.

Oscar stood up in his new socks, and we thought he was about to make a little speech, but all he said was, 'I enjoyed the commotion.'

Ruben said, 'Hear, hear,' and I clapped, and Kite rolled backwards and yelled. Then we ate some biscotti, and Ruben said we should all go home and rest, and then we had to come back for a five o'clock call.

Caramella and I walked home together. I told her Barnaby was back. I didn't tell her about my dad, not yet.

'No way! When did he come?'

'In the middle of the night. He came to see the show.'

'That's amazing. How did he know?'

I told her the whole story.

'God, are you nervous?' she said, grabbing my hand.

'Yeah, are you?'

Caramella didn't have to do anything too acrobatic in the show. Nothing too hard anyway. Only things she felt physically confident doing, like supporting and acting out parts. But still, she was in it. *And* she was the designer.

'Yep, I think so. I can't tell if it's nervousness or excitedness.'

'No. Me neither.' I thought about Kite and about Barnaby and my dad and my mum and love and black swans and noble paintings and thigh stands and I thought there were so many things happening all at once it was no wonder I couldn't tell which feeling was what. Maybe that's just what happens when you grow up; everything gets more so.

I went and tried to nap, but it didn't work. Too many things to think about. So I got that old daisy out of the sock drawer. Maybe there was one thing I could clear up. I stood at the window and pulled the petals off, one by one tossing them into the air, as if I was throwing hankies off a ship in a dramatic farewell scene. When it got near the end I slowed down and looked ahead. I can't help it.
I'm impatient. There were three left.

He loves me . . . He loves me not . . .

He loves me.

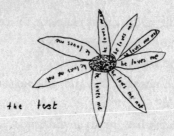

the test

I kept the last petal on and stuck it under my pillow, sentimental fool that I am. Did I believe it? Could I really trust a daisy, after all? And maybe I missed a petal. No, I was going to believe it. I was.

I went into Barnaby's room and I sat on the end of his bed, just like I used to. He was sitting there, leaning up against the wall and playing his guitar.

'Hey, Barn.'

'Yep?'

'So . . . Tell me about your black swan.'

'Lisa,' he said, and put down the guitar.

'Was it all three parts?' I said. He laughed, and his hand stroked his chin and he nodded.

'I guess so. All three, yep. Mind, body and soul. She laughs like a waterfall. And she smells good.'

'You gonna see her again?'

'Hope so. I sure plan to.'

'Does she live in WA?'

'She's thinking of coming here, to visit, maybe study. She's got a job now – maybe when she gets some savings.'

'What does she do?'

'She wants to study.'

'What?'

'Sculpture, I think, or history. She's a vego, like you.'

'What are you going to do, Barn? You going to study, too?'

'I reckon. I wanna study music.'

'So you're in love?'

'Maybe.'

I heaved a big sigh and then he ruffled my hair up, and then we had a tickle fight. (Boy am I glad he never fell in love with someone like Marnie Aitkin.)

Then it was time to go.

'Chookers,' said Barnaby.

'What the hell does that mean?'

He shrugged.

'I dunno. It's just what you say to someone for good luck before a show.'

☆   ☆   ☆

I went and said goodbye to Mum. She was gazing out the kitchen window, with a dreamy, sad look on her face. I'd seen that look so many times, but I'd never really understood it before, never known what kind of sadnesses lurked around inside her.

'I'm going now, Mum.'

She turned towards me and smiled and her face was soft. I went and hugged her. I don't know why I did that. I just

wanted to. I buried my head in her shoulder and closed my
eyes and I could smell the familiar smell of her, the smell of
warmth and comfort and safety and everything that
continued. It was probably about the deepest, quietest, best
smell I knew. I wanted to tell her that, but I didn't. I just
breathed it in. Deep breaths of Mum smell. I whispered in
her shoulder that I knew about Dad and it was okay. She
squeezed me tight and patted my back, and I felt her
nodding. But she didn't speak. I thought maybe she couldn't.
I think she might have been crying, but I didn't look. It was
better like that. It was better to let the feelings just melt
through, direct from one body to another, no translations,
just a big bare sense of us, together. Mum was patting my
back. My eyes were closed. We were there like that for a
very long time.

When I left she came with me to the door and said,
'Break a leg, darling.'

People say funny things to you before you get ready for
a circus.

# Chapter 37

Ruben was seating people, and Mr Zito was taking money, because he's an accountant. Kite, Caramella and I were waiting in the laneway behind the garage, and poor Oscar was all alone, waiting in the dark on the stage. We could hear people coming in and sitting on the chairs. We had put cushions on the floor, too, because we couldn't fit in that many chairs. Caramella kept peeking in the garage door, and running out to the back lane and reporting who was there and how many people.

'Oh my god! Harold Barton is there, and so are Marnie and Aileen. Your brother and mum are in the front row, Cedar, and Ricci's with them. There's about fifty people, I swear. It's packed. Full House!'

That was when I really felt nervous. I kept having to go and wee, and my tummy felt funny. I was thinking about my family, my whole family, being there to watch me. I liked to say that word, *Family*, because now that Barn was here we weren't just a pair, Mum and I. We were a group. Barnaby

had come back to see *me*. That proves we were a real family
with ties and love and history and a dog. Even if there was
no dad, there was still all that. It felt incredibly good to have
a whole family. They were here for me! (Oh yeah, and
Bambi.)

*     *     *

I kept jumping up and down to keep warm. The voices
hushed, and we could see a faint glow coming from
underneath the door. That was our cue. It meant Oscar had
lit up like a lamp and we would be going on in ten seconds.
I looked at Kite. He grabbed my hand and looked straight
ahead at the door. Under his breath he was counting.
Then he dropped my hand and began to open the door.
The music started. We were on.

I didn't look at the audience at first. I was concentrating.
I couldn't bear to look. I could hear Oscar's whistle. Each
time he blew it, I knew what to do — walk fast, change
direction, dive roll over Caramella, she rolls over and over,
Kite walks on his hands, I back into him and hold his ankles,
I bend forward, flipping him up the right way. There is
clapping. I hear Oscar's deep wobbly voice ringing out, only
it sounds almost sturdy now, with just a faint theatrical
tremor . . .

 . . . *often the roundness of life is sacrificed to the rule of the line
which is always progressing upwards and onwards,*

(I climb up on Kite's shoulders. Standing up, I reach higher, as if I want to keep climbing. Kite grips my ankles and I drop my heels.)

*or becoming longer like a track across the desert,*

(I jump down and fall forwards in a straight line as Kite falls backwards. I hold his ankles and Caramella holds mine. Then, one by one, we twist over.)

*or moving faster and faster towards conclusions.*

(At this point, Kite and I roll backwards and press up into handstands. Caramella slides forward on her belly, and we dive roll in time over her from one side to the other, as if she is trapped. We're going faster and faster and the audience is laughing. I'm feeling great. Positively bionic.)

*So this show is a small homage to roundness. In the manner of a circle, it spins around, and like a seed on a windy day, it circles around the places of wonder and slowly comes to settle in the school playground where there are no endings, only beginnings . . .*

(I am cartwheeling, cartwheeling, up onto Kite's shoulders, a perfect helicopter. He lets me down gently and Oscar blows his whistle . . . the playground fun begins.)

First there is the tug of war . . . And then it goes on and on and I don't forget or fall and people are clapping and Oscar is speaking and Kite is flying through the air and people are clapping and there is the handspring and I am feeling high and heavenly and now people are laughing and the whistle blows and Oscar speaks and on and on, I wobble in that balance, but I don't fall, and again Kite is on the trapeze and soaring through the air until it's already the last bit, the best lift, the knee-and-shoulder spring, now me flying and a good landing and more clapping and it's finished and we're all taking a bow and Ruben comes on with us and I can see Oscar's mother and she has tears in her eyes and Ricci is jumping up and down and Barnaby is smiling at me and we're all still holding hands in a line, me and Kite and Oscar and Caramella and Ruben, and I scan through the audience to see who I recognise, and I see Mum, and Barn who has Stinky on his lap, and Tophy Sutton from school, and Hoody Mott and also Hailey and the Lebbos, and Patrick and Aileen Shelby, and Marnie Aitkin who is staring wide-eyed and gobsmacked, and there are the boys, Robert in his lilac shirt and Pablo de la Renta, and there is Harold Barton with his shades on and next to him are his parents, Mr and Mrs Barton, and they are both clapping and I am imagining how I will explain very politely to Mr Barton how we found the skateboard and then how Mr Barton will be embarrassed and sorry for accusing Barnaby and making judgments and he will have to punish his son Harold for lying and causing trouble and Harold will be made to apologise to Barnaby who will just shrug it off anyway and Harold will feel like a real loser for a little while, but I won't gloat, well maybe just quietly to myself . . . And now people are coming onto the stage and I see my mum and she is shaking hands with Ruben and Ruben doesn't seem shy at

all, he seems strong, and my mum is smiling and being
friendly to him, and then she's giving me a hug and then
she's even hugging Kite and he's blushing and Barnaby is
ruffling my hair and I don't even care, and I wonder if we
made enough money for Ricci's dog Bambi, and Mr and
Mrs Zito have their hands flying about and Caramella looks
like an angel and Oscar's mother is dabbing at her eyes with
a Kleenex and Oscar is sitting down on a chair and she has
her hand on his head and people are talking to him and he
looks as if he is holding court and Barnaby is introducing
me to Mrs Mozart (the truck driver's wife) and she is
gushing on and holding her kid's hand saying what a show,
amazing, wish Ed could have seen it too, and does anyone
give lessons because her children wanted to learn, and before
I can answer, Kite is standing right in front of me and Stinky
is between us wagging his tail and letting off little barks, and
we smile, and we are standing very close to each other and
I feel this enormous funny feeling, *the* funny feeling, and my
skin is getting zapped by it and I am thinking, *I know what is
about to happen.* I rock up onto my toes and a thought flies
through me, just a red ribbon of thought going – *Cedar, as
soon as you think you know how things will go, life is liable to
scribble a little detour right over the path you thought you were on,
and lo and behold, there could be one hundred low flying albatrosses
about to swoop in and take Kite flying away to Siberia with them,
just when you think he is about to kiss you.*

So I am quickly pretending I don't know what is about to happen.

And I am letting my eyes close and Kite is leaning down towards me and I am balancing on my toes and I don't see one single albatross for miles.

*nearly one hundred albatrosses in a bath*

## AcroBRATS save Bambi

Last week a group of four young performers gave a benefit debut performance (Volatile) which not only impressed audiences but succeeded in raising enough money to pay for a neighbour's dog's operation. The group, directed by Ruben Freeman, formerly of Circus Berzerkus, is thrilled with the response and plans to keep training and developing skills. Ruben claims that the young performers themselves came up with the material and he simply 'pulled it into shape'. He will be also conducting classes in circus skills for all ages and all levels of experience. For enquiries please call soon as classes are filling up quickly. 9380 4785.